THE FIFTH MUSKETEER

JUSTINE & RON FONTES

ILLUSTRATED BY DYLAN MECONIS

GRAPHIC UNIVERSE™ • MINNEAPOLIS • NEW YORK

Story by Justine and Ron Fontes

Pencils and inks by Dylan Meconis

Coloring by Jenn Manley Lee

Lettering by Marshall Dillon

Copyright © 2012 by Lerner Publishing Group, Inc.

Graphic Universe™ is a trademark and Twisted Journeys® is a registered trademark of Lerner Publishing Group, Inc.

Graphic Universe™
A division of Lerner Publishing Group, Inc.
241 First Avenue North
Minneapolis, MN 55401 U.S.A.

Website address: www.lernerbooks.com

Main body text set in Myriad Tilt Bold 14/16.
Typeface provided by Adobe Systems.

Library of Congress Cataloging-in-Publication Data

Fontes, Justine.
      The fifth Musketeer / by Justine & Ron Fontes ; illustrated by Dylan Meconis.
          p.   cm. — (Twisted journeys ; #19)
      Summary: Against the odds, a young peasant in seventeenth-century France strives to join the famous swordsmen known as the Musketeers, and the reader is asked to make choices throughout the story to determine the outcome.
      ISBN 978-0-7613-4594-7 (lib. bdg. : alk. paper)
      1. Plot-your-own stories. 2. Graphic novels. [1. Graphic novels. 2. Adventure and adventurers—Fiction. 3. Characters in literature—Fiction. 4. Paris (France)—History—17th century—Fiction. 5. France—History—Louis XIII, 1610-1643—Fiction. 6. Plot-your-own stories.] I. Fontes, Ron. II. Meconis, Dylan, ill. III. Title.
PZ7.7.F66Fif 2012
741.5'973—dc23   2011021744

Manufactured in the United States of America
1 – DP – 12/31/11

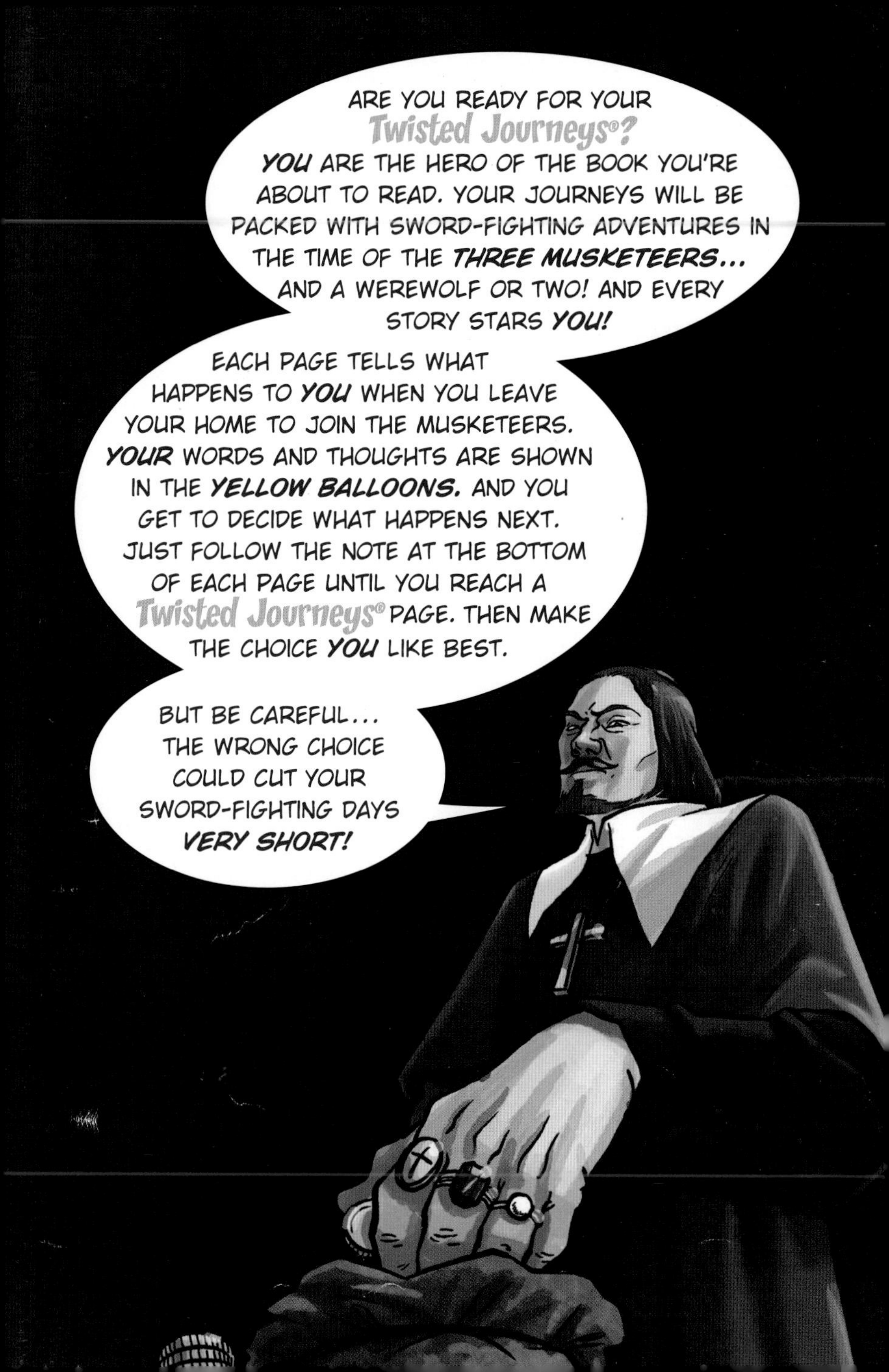
ARE YOU READY FOR YOUR Twisted Journeys®? YOU ARE THE HERO OF THE BOOK YOU'RE ABOUT TO READ. YOUR JOURNEYS WILL BE PACKED WITH SWORD-FIGHTING ADVENTURES IN THE TIME OF THE THREE MUSKETEERS... AND A WEREWOLF OR TWO! AND EVERY STORY STARS YOU!
EACH PAGE TELLS WHAT HAPPENS TO YOU WHEN YOU LEAVE YOUR HOME TO JOIN THE MUSKETEERS. YOUR WORDS AND THOUGHTS ARE SHOWN IN THE YELLOW BALLOONS. AND YOU GET TO DECIDE WHAT HAPPENS NEXT. JUST FOLLOW THE NOTE AT THE BOTTOM OF EACH PAGE UNTIL YOU REACH A Twisted Journeys® PAGE. THEN MAKE THE CHOICE YOU LIKE BEST.
BUT BE CAREFUL... THE WRONG CHOICE COULD CUT YOUR SWORD-FIGHTING DAYS VERY SHORT!

You have no right to want to be a Musketeer. Your family is not noble. But your parents have always taught you that nobility comes from character, not birth. And ever since you found the rapier hidden under the floorboards in the barn, you have wanted to prove you have what it takes to be a Musketeer!

The sword comes with a story, and a scar. Up until you were twelve, you believed the scar marring Father's face came from a robber's knife. The robber attacked a nobleman near your village in southern France. Father intervened with the bravery and ferocity for which all Gascons, the people from the region of Gascogne, are famous. His reward was the scar, but also the gift of a fertile farm from the nobleman, who wished to remain anonymous.

But where had Father learned to read, write, and fight with a sword? The average Gascon farmer never learns such skills. What really happened?

GO ON TO THE NEXT PAGE.

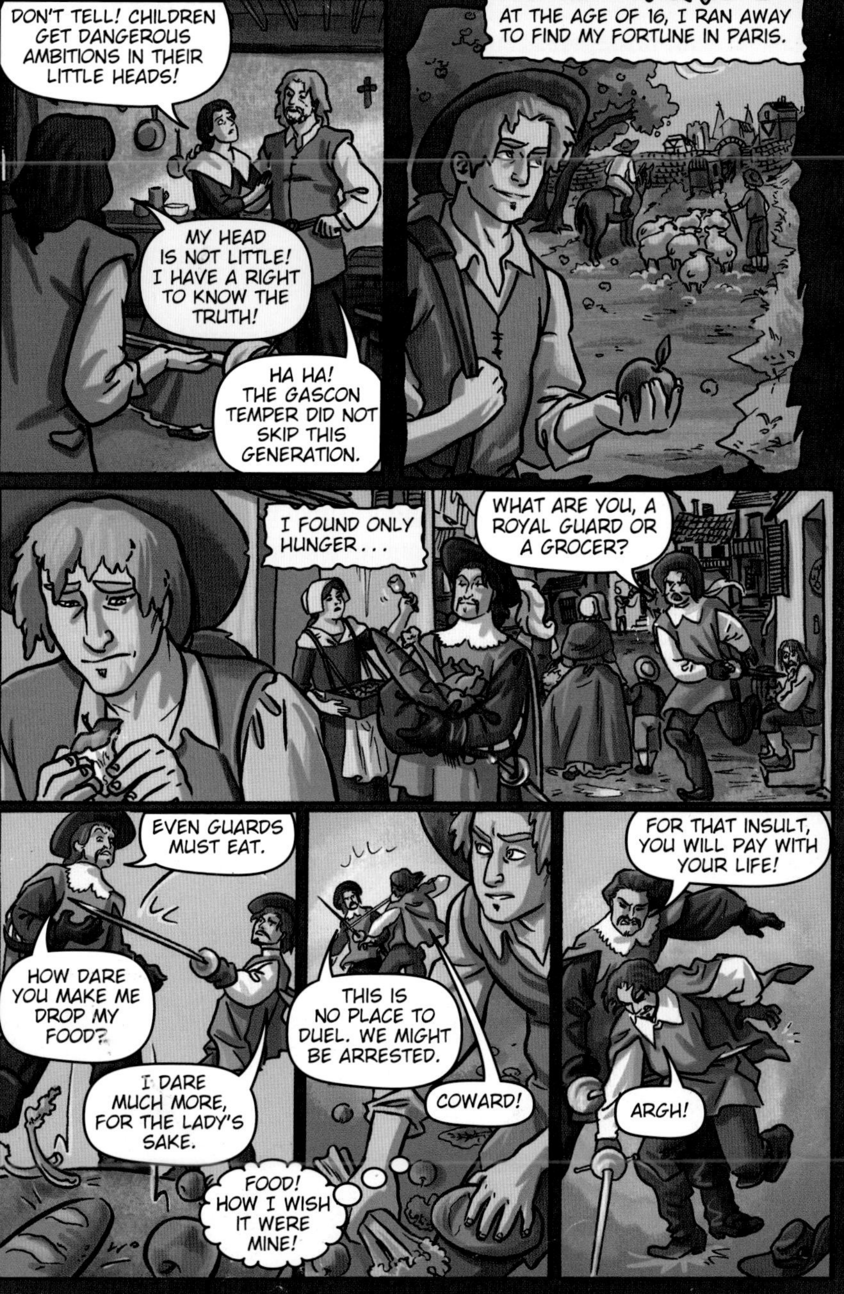

DON'T TELL! CHILDREN GET DANGEROUS AMBITIONS IN THEIR LITTLE HEADS!
MY HEAD IS NOT LITTLE! I HAVE A RIGHT TO KNOW THE TRUTH!
HA HA! THE GASCON TEMPER DID NOT SKIP THIS GENERATION.
AT THE AGE OF 16, I RAN AWAY TO FIND MY FORTUNE IN PARIS.
I FOUND ONLY HUNGER...
WHAT ARE YOU, A ROYAL GUARD OR A GROCER?
EVEN GUARDS MUST EAT.
HOW DARE YOU MAKE ME DROP MY FOOD?
I DARE MUCH MORE, FOR THE LADY'S SAKE.
THIS IS NO PLACE TO DUEL. WE MIGHT BE ARRESTED.
COWARD!
FOOD! HOW I WISH IT WERE MINE!
FOR THAT INSULT, YOU WILL PAY WITH YOUR LIFE!
ARGH!

GO ON TO THE NEXT PAGE.

Your father was tempted by the fallen food, but he resisted. This impressed the victor, Monsieur de Treville. You gasp, because even a country bumpkin like you recognizes the name of the captain of the Musketeers!

Father explains that Treville was not yet captain. But the young guard saw promise in the hungry-but-honest boy and let Father become his lackey.

Father persuaded Treville to teach him everything about swordsmanship and the other gentlemanly arts. Then one day during a fierce battle, Treville was badly wounded. To protect his master, Father put on a Musketeer cassock and fought in Treville's place. When his highborn enemy found out he was fighting a peasant, he gave Father the scar.

From that day on, Treville could not look at your father without remembering that his servant had more honor than he did. Grateful but humiliated, Treville sent Father away, giving him the farm on the condition that he hide his sword forever.

GO ON TO THE NEXT PAGE.

Now that you know the truth about
your father's background,

WILL YOU . . .

. . . beg him to teach you as Treville taught him,
so that you can become a Musketeer?
TURN TO PAGE 14.

. . . listen to your mother's heartfelt pleas to
pursue a less dangerous course?
TURN TO PAGE 35.

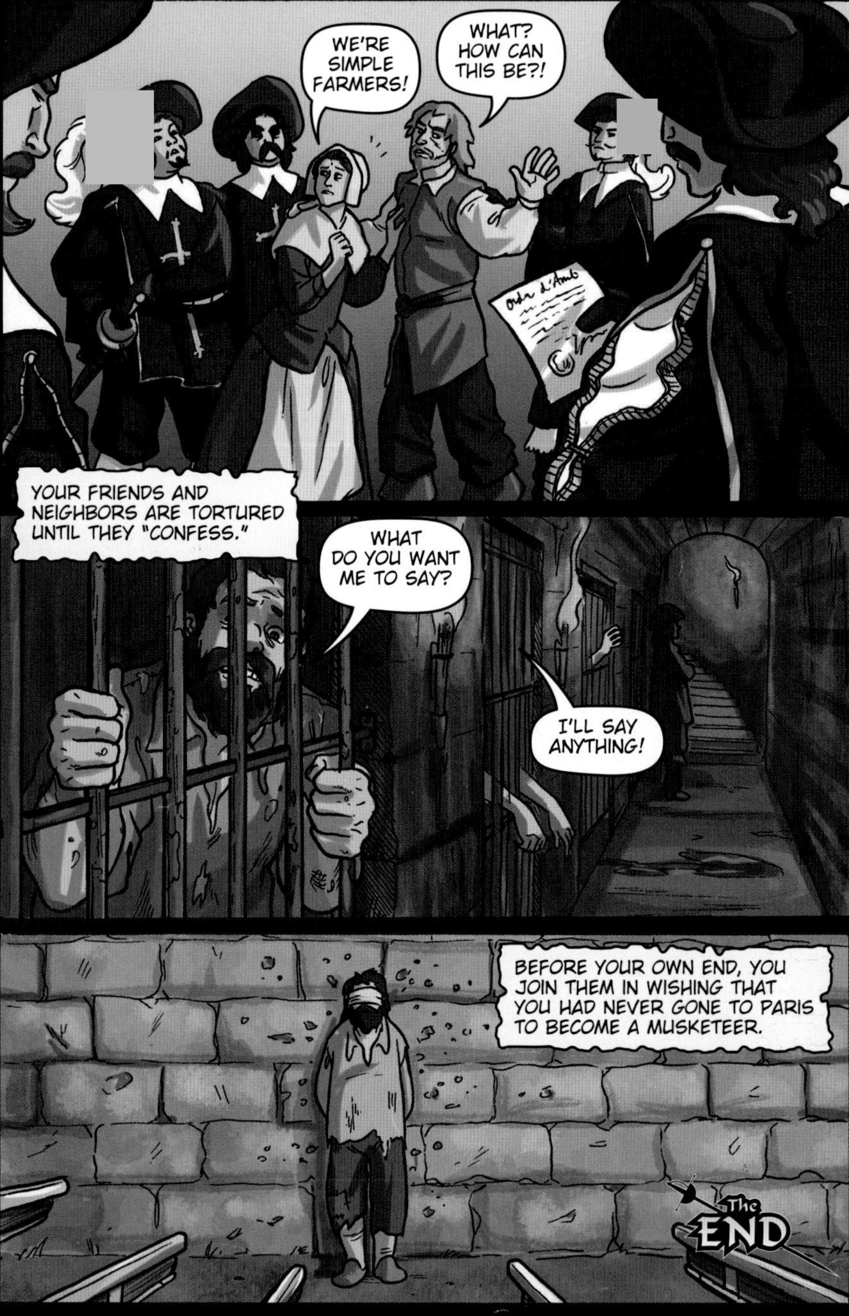
WE'RE SIMPLE FARMERS!
WHAT? HOW CAN THIS BE?!
YOUR FRIENDS AND NEIGHBORS ARE TORTURED UNTIL THEY "CONFESS."
WHAT DO YOU WANT ME TO SAY?
I'LL SAY ANYTHING!
BEFORE YOUR OWN END, YOU JOIN THEM IN WISHING THAT YOU HAD NEVER GONE TO PARIS TO BECOME A MUSKETEER.
The END

When she hears your request for a potion of power, the witch takes your coins in exchange for a vial. "Drink this to become as strong as a wolf!"

Outside, Giles tells you he has found a smokehouse full of meat at a cottage that has no livestock, plus several wolf skins. He tastes the witch's potion and shudders. "That poison could drive a man mad. Even convince him he's a wolf!"

With this evidence, you return to the duke. He commands his best men to help you capture both the crone and her cronies.

When you return with the prisoners, you receive a rich reward. The duke sends a letter to Treville, and the King himself commands that you be admitted into the Musketeers!

You finally join the distinguished company of Musketeers, in which you do many famous deeds. But you never lose the nickname Porthos gives you on your first day as a Musketeer when he shouts, "Hurrah, Wolfy!"

THE END

Not knowing what else to do, you pray with your fellow soldiers who are hoping for a miracle. This helps them face the battle with courage.

During the battle, a cannonball shatters your leg! You survive, but this hurts too much to be a miracle.

The nobleman whose army you are serving in rewards you generously. You build a home near your family's farm. Because of your bad leg, you will never be able to become a Musketeer.

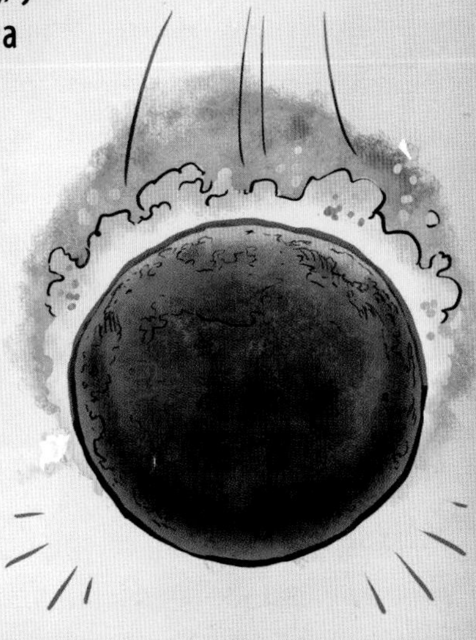

Local children ask to hear your war stories. You do not have the heart to fill their heads with dreams of glory. Like many veterans, your dreams are full of memories of the battle.

You follow news about the war as it flares up all over Europe. To your amazement, it does not end until 1648! Who could have imagined there would be a "Thirty Years War"?

THE END

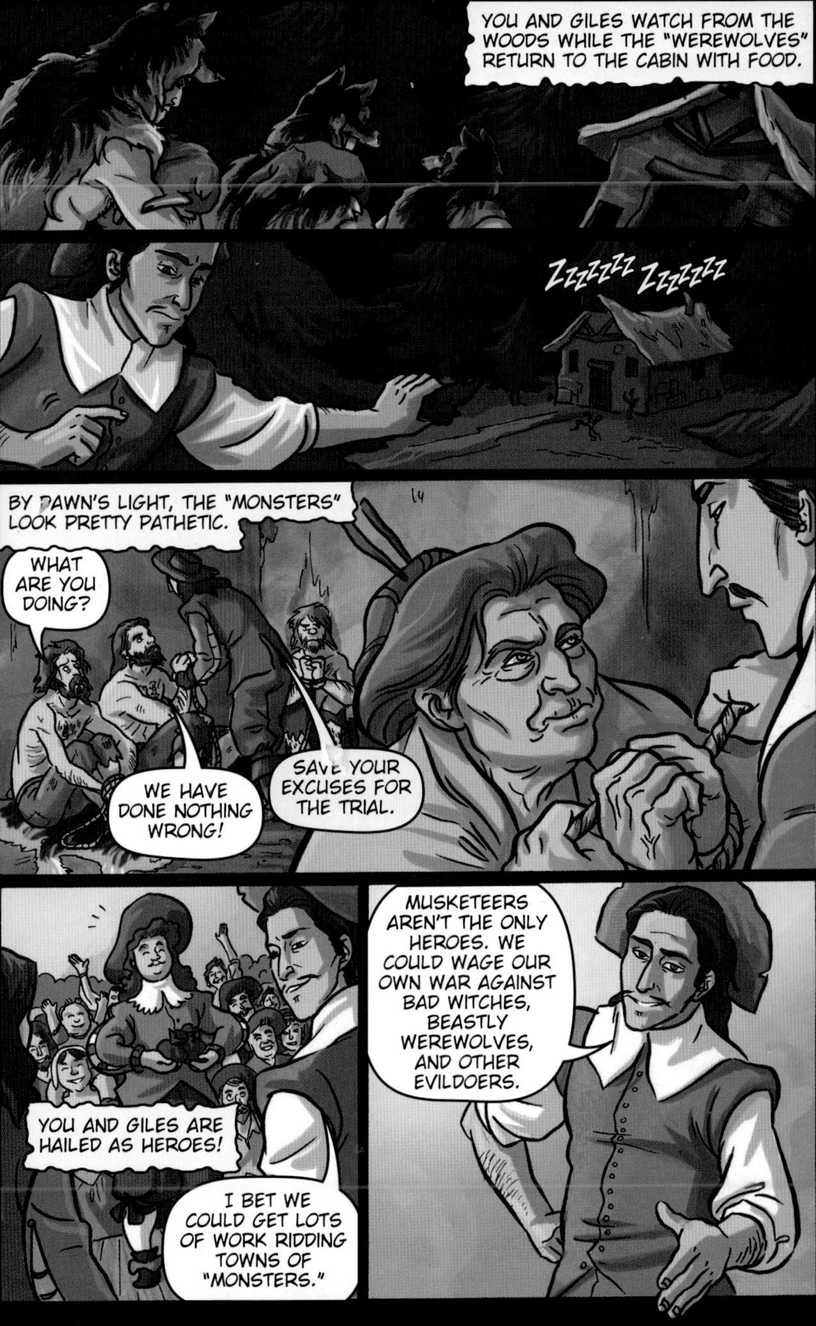

YOU AND GILES WATCH FROM THE WOODS WHILE THE "WEREWOLVES" RETURN TO THE CABIN WITH FOOD.
Zzzzzzz Zzzzzzz
BY DAWN'S LIGHT, THE "MONSTERS" LOOK PRETTY PATHETIC.
WHAT ARE YOU DOING?
WE HAVE DONE NOTHING WRONG!
SAVE YOUR EXCUSES FOR THE TRIAL.
YOU AND GILES ARE HAILED AS HEROES!
I BET WE COULD GET LOTS OF WORK RIDDING TOWNS OF "MONSTERS."
MUSKETEERS AREN'T THE ONLY HEROES. WE COULD WAGE OUR OWN WAR AGAINST BAD WITCHES, BEASTLY WEREWOLVES, AND OTHER EVILDOERS.

GO ON TO THE NEXT PAGE.

WILL YOU . . .

. . . take Giles up on his offer to become
a "witch hunter"?
TURN TO PAGE 47.

. . . continue with your plan to become
a Musketeer?
TURN TO PAGE 16.

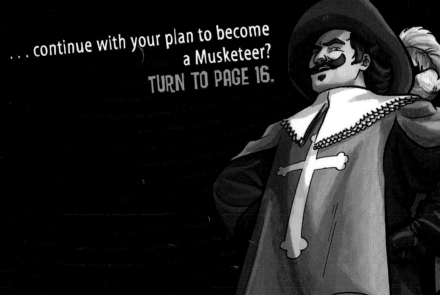

Your career as a diplomat turns out to be quite adventurous. Your Musketeer talents aren't wasted during your travels in France and foreign lands.

Your sword fights off many attacks from bandits and would-be assassins. But your greatest victories come from your ability to see situations from the enemy's point of view.

Whenever possible, you find peaceful solutions. When war is inevitable, your understanding of the enemy's state of mind helps France achieve victory.

In reward for this, King Louis XIII gives you a title and lands. You invite your old rival St. Pierre to the celebration. After all, without his teasing, you wouldn't have achieved all your success!

THE END

You think Father is exaggerating until the drills begin. Your thighs burn like fire. Father just says, "Again, again!"

You are never free to play with your siblings. All you do is parry and thrust. Yet despite occasional cuts and many bruises, you love sword fighting!

Father insists you also learn to speak a smattering of every European language, know Latin, and be able to draw. A Musketeer might fight in foreign lands, so you submit to language lessons. "But," you ask, "how is *drawing* necessary?"

"Because it helps you see precisely and appreciate art, and it is something every gentleman knows," Father replies.

Then you find a forgotten book in Father's collection. It contains many simple line drawings and instructions for turning a lantern and a piece of glass into a tracing box. Those might get you through your drawing lessons quickly and easily.

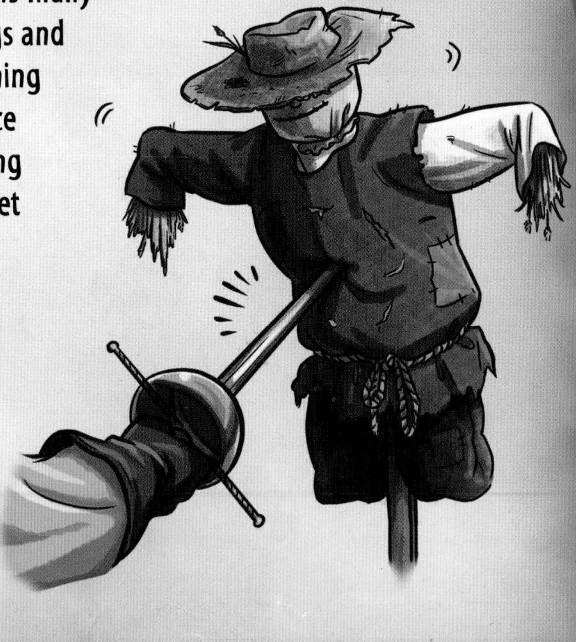

GO ON TO THE NEXT PAGE.

WILL YOU . . .

. . . build the box and hide it from Father, because a clever Musketeer sometimes takes a shortcut?
TURN TO PAGE 19.

. . . build the box but show it to Father?
TURN TO PAGE 22.

. . . copy the drawings on your own, because tracing is not the same as learning to draw and a Musketeer never cheats?
TURN TO PAGE 42.

You have every intention of someday becoming a Musketeer. But first you must testify at the trial for the witch and her werewolves.

The judge is impressed by the clarity of your testimony. He asks if you have ever considered studying the law. You tell him that you must be a Musketeer. He shrugs and says, "You are too young to know your calling for certain. I will lend you some books. There's no harm in reading."

You are surprised to find the law fascinating! Truly, the pen is mightier than the sword. Eventually you realize that you have a talent that cannot be denied.

You become a lawyer, fighting for justice with words. In the greatest case of your distinguished career, you save the life of a Musketeer falsely accused of murder. Captain de Treville himself leads the company in cheering your name.

THE END

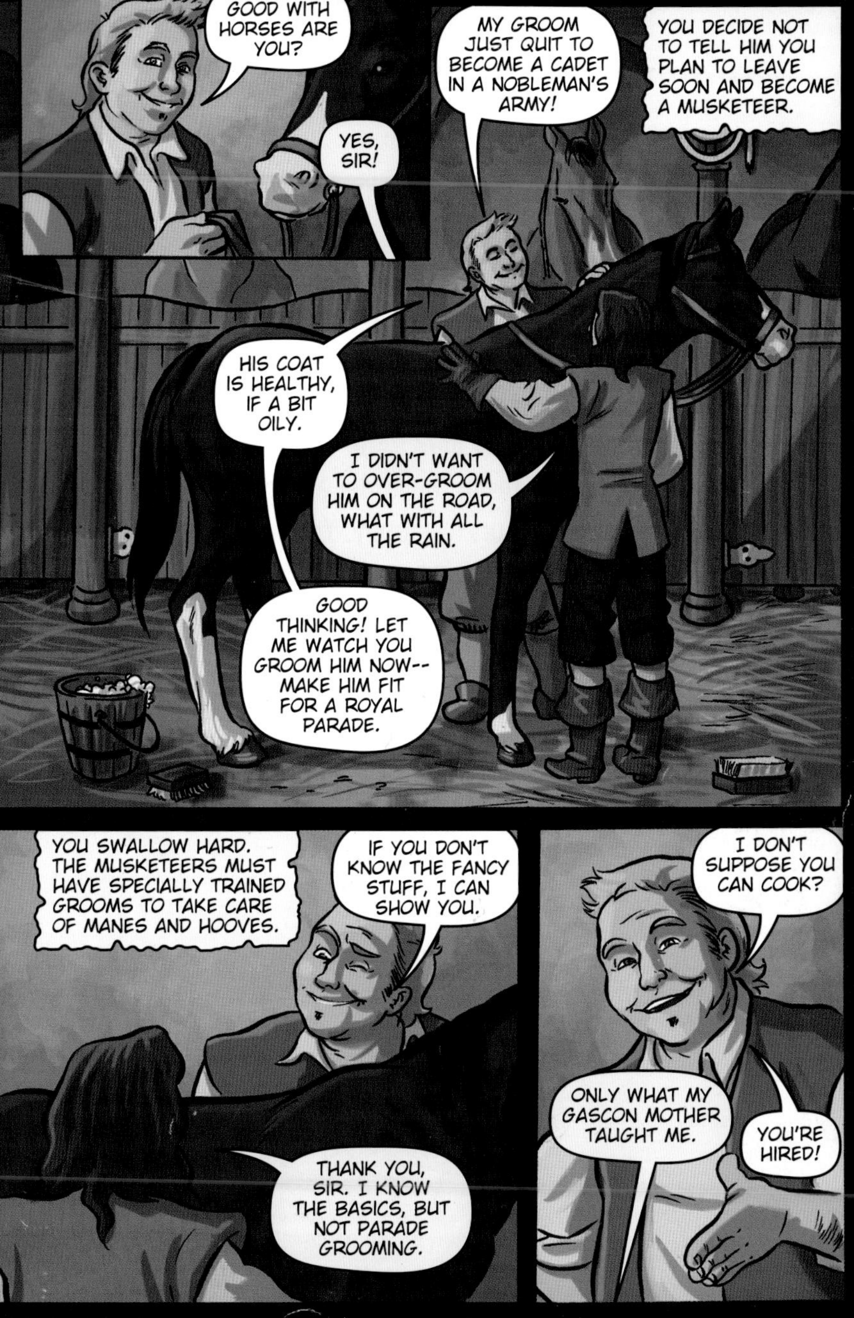
GOOD WITH HORSES ARE YOU?
YES, SIR!
MY GROOM JUST QUIT TO BECOME A CADET IN A NOBLEMAN'S ARMY!
YOU DECIDE NOT TO TELL HIM YOU PLAN TO LEAVE SOON AND BECOME A MUSKETEER.
HIS COAT IS HEALTHY, IF A BIT OILY.
I DIDN'T WANT TO OVER-GROOM HIM ON THE ROAD, WHAT WITH ALL THE RAIN.
GOOD THINKING! LET ME WATCH YOU GROOM HIM NOW--MAKE HIM FIT FOR A ROYAL PARADE.
YOU SWALLOW HARD. THE MUSKETEERS MUST HAVE SPECIALLY TRAINED GROOMS TO TAKE CARE OF MANES AND HOOVES.
IF YOU DON'T KNOW THE FANCY STUFF, I CAN SHOW YOU.
THANK YOU, SIR. I KNOW THE BASICS, BUT NOT PARADE GROOMING.
I DON'T SUPPOSE YOU CAN COOK?
ONLY WHAT MY GASCON MOTHER TAUGHT ME.
YOU'RE HIRED!

GO ON TO THE NEXT PAGE.

"My name's Seamus O'Riley, but everyone calls me Spurs because I refuse to use them," the Irish stable owner announces.

You grin, because you and Pinky don't like spurs, either.

Spurs adds, "I'm tired of my own cooking. I'll be glad for anything you can make out of what's in the larder."

Spurs sets up a bed for you near the kitchen fire. He lives in an apartment above the barn. "It's nothing fancy," he says. "But I'm here if the horses need me."

You find some beans in the larder and cook Mother's cassoulet. Spurs devours it happily. You have the strangest feeling of coming home.

The next day, you and Pinky ride to Musketeer headquarters to meet Monsieur de Treville.

18

TURN TO PAGE 74.

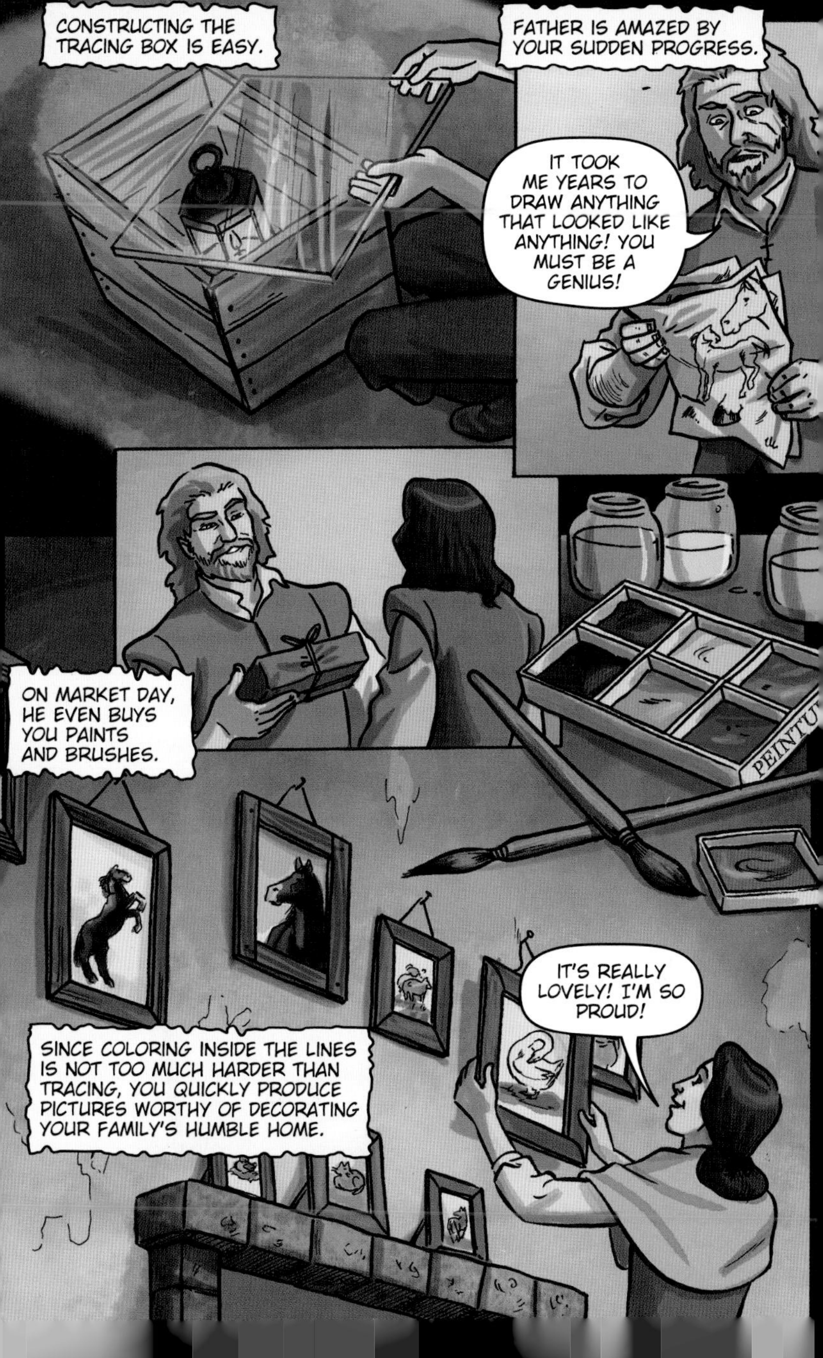
CONSTRUCTING THE TRACING BOX IS EASY.
FATHER IS AMAZED BY YOUR SUDDEN PROGRESS.
IT TOOK ME YEARS TO DRAW ANYTHING THAT LOOKED LIKE ANYTHING! YOU MUST BE A GENIUS!
ON MARKET DAY, HE EVEN BUYS YOU PAINTS AND BRUSHES.
PEINTU
SINCE COLORING INSIDE THE LINES IS NOT TOO MUCH HARDER THAN TRACING, YOU QUICKLY PRODUCE PICTURES WORTHY OF DECORATING YOUR FAMILY'S HUMBLE HOME.
IT'S REALLY LOVELY! I'M SO PROUD!

Knowing that your family's compliments are based on false achievements hardens your heart. Father can teach you nothing more. It's time you went to Paris.

You use your tracing box to copy Father's handwriting and create a letter of introduction to his former master. In it, you hint about the scar and Treville's pride. You claim the right to become a Musketeer without the usual training period elsewhere.

Since your family will search for you unless they know you are safe, you leave a note with the perfect lie: you've gone to Paris to become an artist's apprentice. Mother won't worry, thinking you'll be safely cleaning a maestro's brushes. And Father won't think of contacting Monsieur de Treville on his own.

As you sneak off into the night, your brilliance delights you even more than the silvery moon.

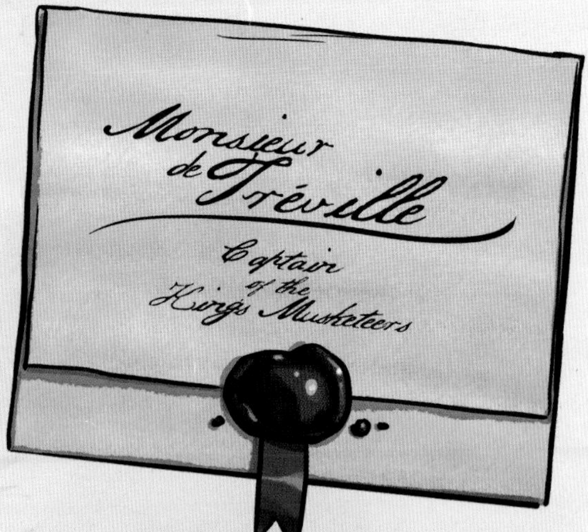
Monsieur
de Tréville
Captain
of the
King's Musketeers

GO ON TO THE NEXT PAGE.

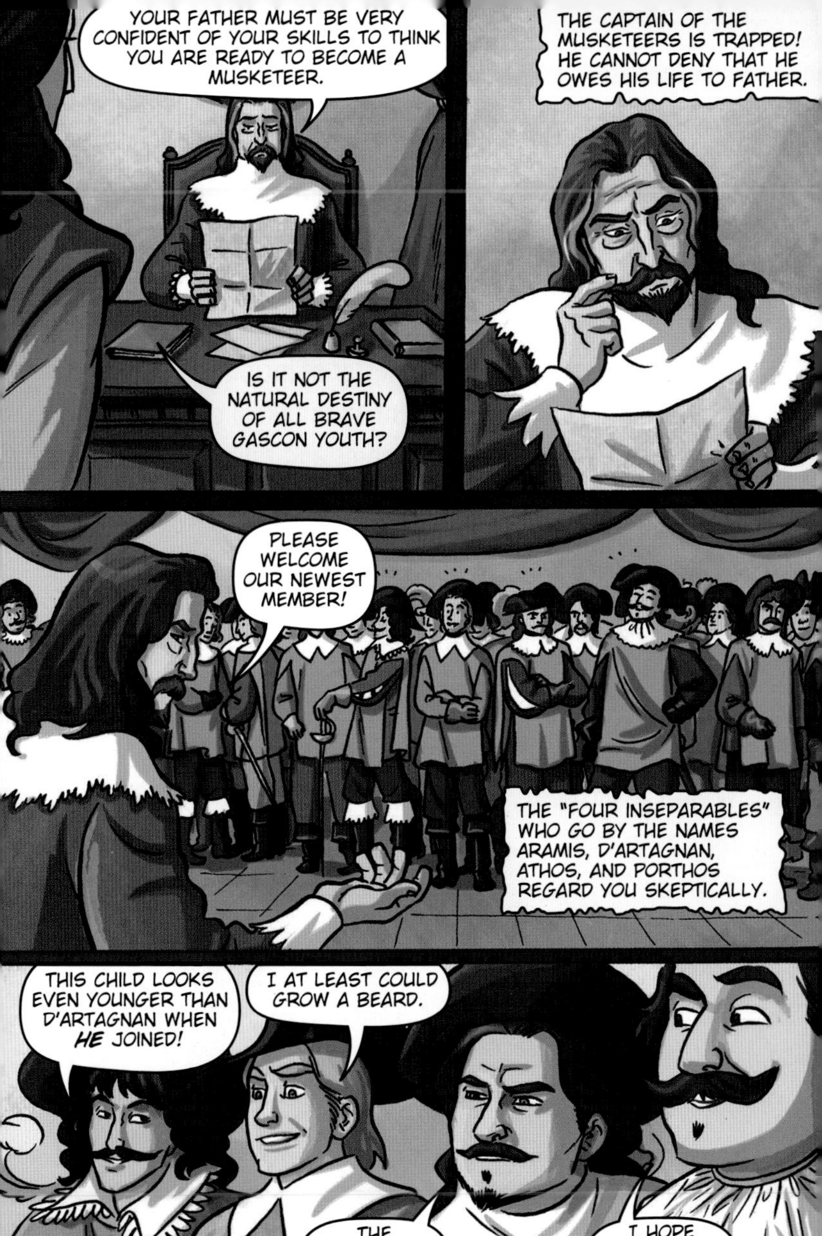
YOUR FATHER MUST BE VERY CONFIDENT OF YOUR SKILLS TO THINK YOU ARE READY TO BECOME A MUSKETEER.
IS IT NOT THE NATURAL DESTINY OF ALL BRAVE GASCON YOUTH?
THE CAPTAIN OF THE MUSKETEERS IS TRAPPED! HE CANNOT DENY THAT HE OWES HIS LIFE TO FATHER.
PLEASE WELCOME OUR NEWEST MEMBER!
THE "FOUR INSEPARABLES" WHO GO BY THE NAMES ARAMIS, D'ARTAGNAN, ATHOS, AND PORTHOS REGARD YOU SKEPTICALLY.
THIS CHILD LOOKS EVEN YOUNGER THAN D'ARTAGNAN WHEN HE JOINED!
I AT LEAST COULD GROW A BEARD.
THE CHILD MUST BE VERY WELL CONNECTED.
I HOPE THIS ONE LIKES TO LOSE AT CARDS!

Father admires your honesty. The box revives his interest in painting, and you help him build frames for his artwork.

Father earns extra money selling art and frames along with his produce. He asks you to stay in business with him. You are tempted, but you *must* be a Musketeer!

On your eighteenth birthday, Father gives you half of the business profits plus a letter of introduction to Treville. You could use the money to take a coach to Paris. Or you could save your coins and ride the farm's old plow horse, Pinky. Father is happy to let you take Pinky. He even warns, with a smile, "Don't let *anyone* tease you about his silly name. Even horses have honor!"

Pinky has been part of your Musketeer training, as you learned to fight from horseback. Riding into the big city on an old horse might make you seem like a country bumpkin. But even horses have feelings. Will Pinky be heartbroken if you leave him behind?

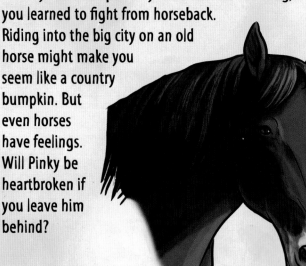

GO ON TO THE NEXT PAGE.

WILL YOU . . .

. . . ride Pinky to Paris to share in your
Musketeer adventure?
TURN TO PAGE 33.

. . . leave Pinky safely at home on the farm?
TURN TO PAGE 45.

Luckily, of all the Musketeers, St. Pierre has the weakest skill with a sword. You suspect he became a Musketeer because of influence and wealth instead of ability.

Soon you are tiring him out! With each attack, you get closer to victory. But you wonder if you will have the courage to make a killing blow. You remind yourself of his insults. Doesn't this sneering snob deserve whatever he gets?

The sight of a man in a red robe catches your eye. You hear someone murmur, "Richelieu!"

St. Pierre stops fighting. You turn to see Cardinal Richelieu's furious face. Richelieu, the King's minister, hates duels, because his brother died in one. The cardinal convinced King Louis to outlaw dueling, but the King often pardons offenders.

However, Richelieu decides to make an example of you!

24

TURN TO PAGE 75.

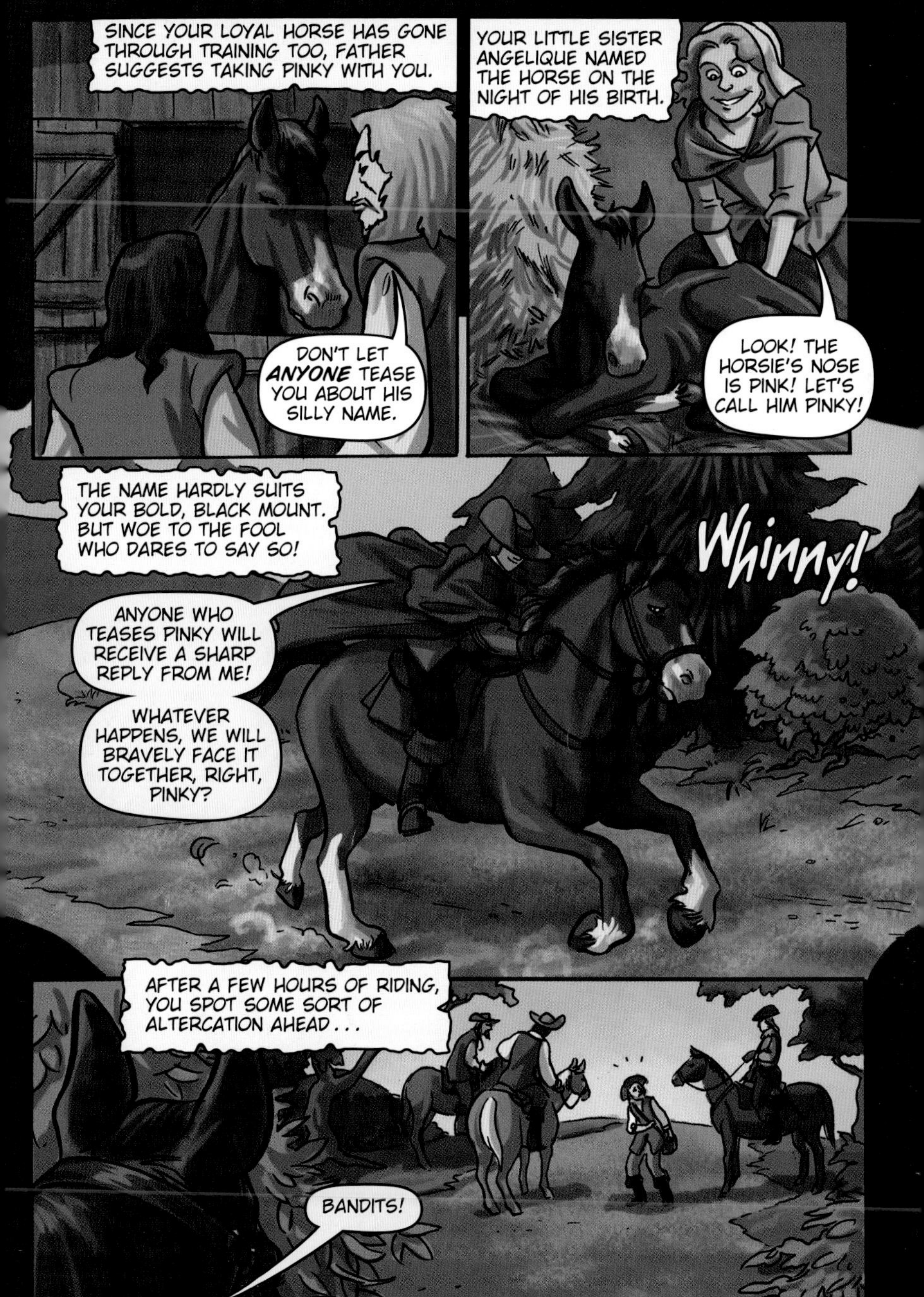
SINCE YOUR LOYAL HORSE HAS GONE THROUGH TRAINING TOO, FATHER SUGGESTS TAKING PINKY WITH YOU.
DON'T LET ANYONE TEASE YOU ABOUT HIS SILLY NAME.
YOUR LITTLE SISTER ANGELIQUE NAMED THE HORSE ON THE NIGHT OF HIS BIRTH.
LOOK! THE HORSIE'S NOSE IS PINK! LET'S CALL HIM PINKY!
THE NAME HARDLY SUITS YOUR BOLD, BLACK MOUNT. BUT WOE TO THE FOOL WHO DARES TO SAY SO!
Whinny!
ANYONE WHO TEASES PINKY WILL RECEIVE A SHARP REPLY FROM ME!
WHATEVER HAPPENS, WE WILL BRAVELY FACE IT TOGETHER, RIGHT, PINKY?
AFTER A FEW HOURS OF RIDING, YOU SPOT SOME SORT OF ALTERCATION AHEAD . . .
BANDITS!

GO ON TO THE NEXT PAGE.

A musketeer must be brave,
no matter what the odds. A victory
on the road will make a great story to tell
Monsieur de Treville when you arrive in Paris.

WILL YOU . . .

. . . boldly ride to the rescue?
TURN TO PAGE 37.

. . . try to trick the robbers?
TURN TO PAGE 29.

Rather than beg from Treville, you decide to work your way home performing odd jobs. Since you have nothing left for anyone to steal except your sword, you feel carefree.

The languages Father made you learn help you assist other travelers. You befriend an English merchant and become his bodyguard. When he offers to take you back to England, you agree!

You decide to be a "free lance." You visit Italy, Spain, and Germany, working as a teacher, translator, and fencing instructor. You do not find fame or fortune. But you do lead a long and interesting life.

Your only regret is that your freelance adventurer's life never provides you with steady companions or longtime friends. Sometimes you wish you had someone with whom you could shout the Musketeer cheer of "All for one and one for all!"

THE END

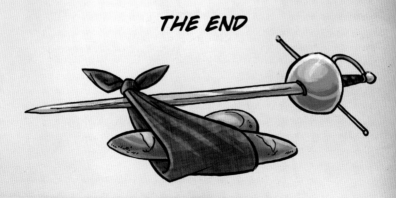

The dream seems like a warning that asking for help will bring trouble to your parents and village. Instead of writing the letter, you draw a plum tree to remind you of the farm. Plum harvests meant picnics, pies, swimming, and other summer fun.

When the priest comes to comfort you before your execution, he asks if you have a vision of heaven. You point to the plum tree.

As you march bravely to the gallows, the crowd sounds like the buzzing of bees among plum blossoms. You feel strangely happy knowing you are protecting the place you love.

When your letters stop arriving at the farm, your family will fear that the worst has happened to you. But they will also get on with their lives, like the bees in the plum blossoms.

THE END

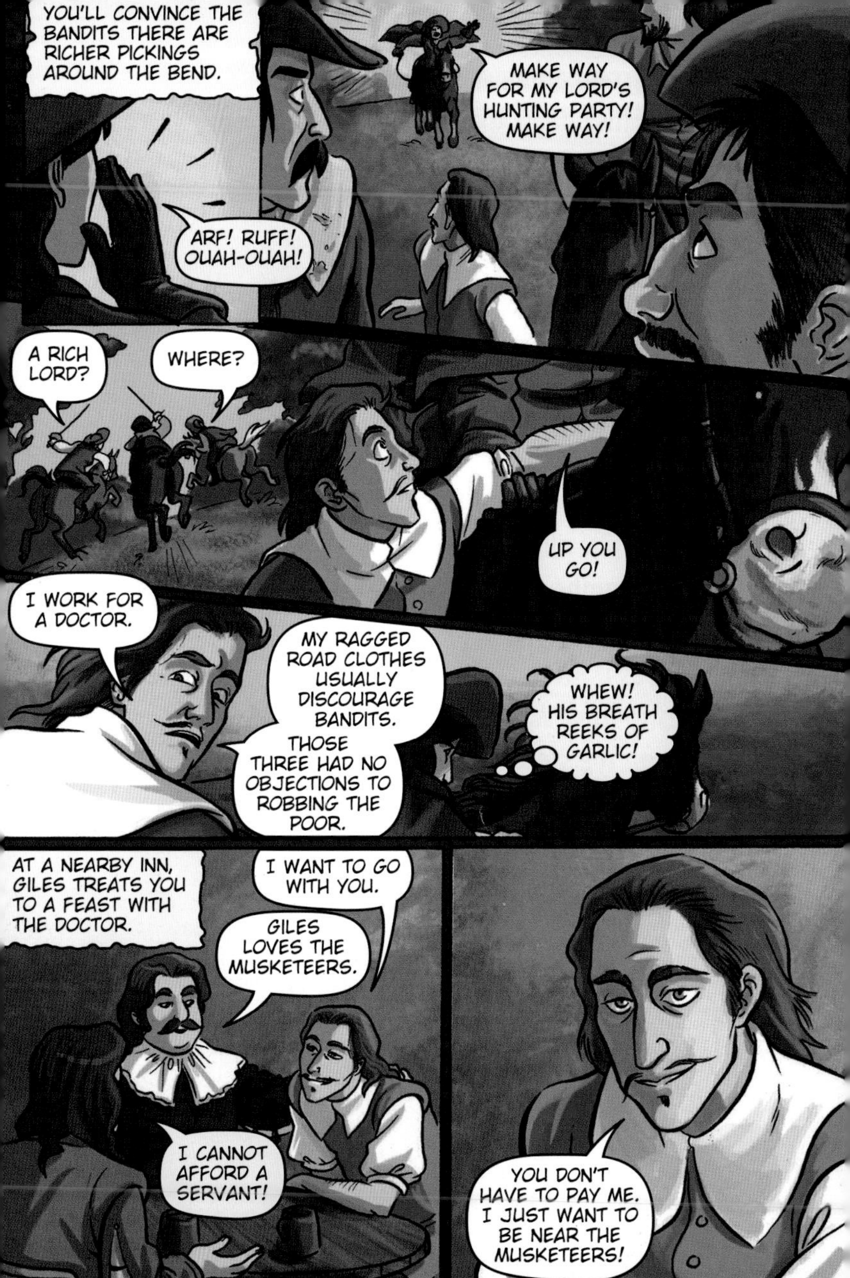

YOU'LL CONVINCE THE BANDITS THERE ARE RICHER PICKINGS AROUND THE BEND.
ARF! RUFF! OUAH-OUAH!
MAKE WAY FOR MY LORD'S HUNTING PARTY! MAKE WAY!
A RICH LORD?
WHERE?
UP YOU GO!
I WORK FOR A DOCTOR.
MY RAGGED ROAD CLOTHES USUALLY DISCOURAGE BANDITS.
THOSE THREE HAD NO OBJECTIONS TO ROBBING THE POOR.
WHEW! HIS BREATH REEKS OF GARLIC!
AT A NEARBY INN, GILES TREATS YOU TO A FEAST WITH THE DOCTOR.
I WANT TO GO WITH YOU.
GILES LOVES THE MUSKETEERS.
I CANNOT AFFORD A SERVANT!
YOU DON'T HAVE TO PAY ME. I JUST WANT TO BE NEAR THE MUSKETEERS!

Having a companion who shares your excitement about the Musketeers makes for a pleasant journey. You fret about never having held a musket. Giles has seen the wounds they inflict and urges you to stay behind the firearm—not in front of it.

In Paris, Giles helps you find Treville's hotel. Many Musketeers mill around the captain's courtyard. Shyness stops you in your tracks so abruptly someone bumps into your back! The giant Musketeer behind you exclaims, "Watch where you're going!"

You mutter, "I'm terribly sorry. I've come to meet Monsieur de Treville."

The man laughs—an insult! You reach for your rapier. He laughs louder. "You're as hot-tempered as D'Artagnan!" Then he waves to three Musketeers lounging on the steps. "Another young Gascon wants to join us, gentlemen."

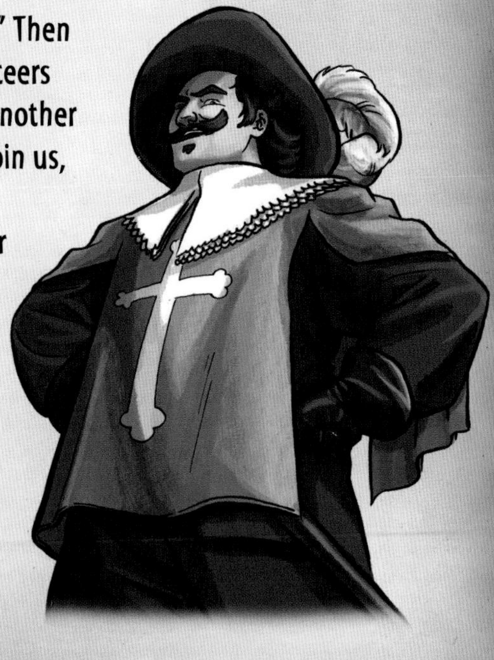

These must be the "four inseparables," the heroes named Athos, Aramis, D'Artagnan, and the gigantic Porthos! Porthos points to a room on the first floor. "That is Treville's office."

TURN TO PAGE 51.

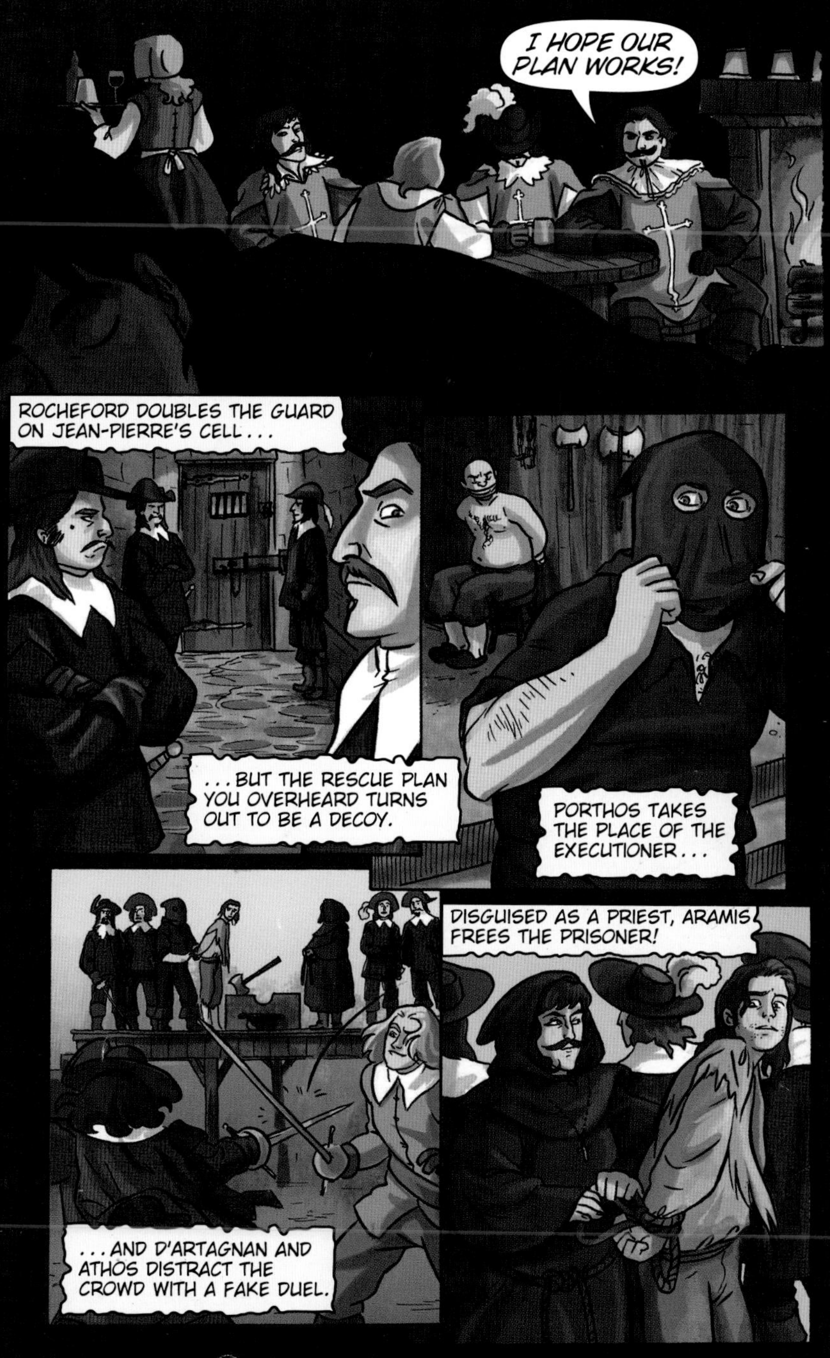
I HOPE OUR PLAN WORKS!
ROCHEFORD DOUBLES THE GUARD ON JEAN-PIERRE'S CELL . . .
. . . BUT THE RESCUE PLAN YOU OVERHEARD TURNS OUT TO BE A DECOY.
PORTHOS TAKES THE PLACE OF THE EXECUTIONER . . .
. . . AND D'ARTAGNAN AND ATHOS DISTRACT THE CROWD WITH A FAKE DUEL.
DISGUISED AS A PRIEST, ARAMIS FREES THE PRISONER!

TURN TO PAGE 102.

The injury to his arm increases your attacker's fury. He parries with so much force, you nearly lose your weapon.

You cannot lose your first battle as a Musketeer! You attack with renewed energy. The enemy steps away from your blow once, then twice, then falls for your fake and steps into your blade instead of away from it. Father would be so proud! But as your enemy falls to the ground, you feel suddenly exhausted and confused. While you are distracted, you're attacked from behind.

The coach doors open and more Musketeers pile out. The King isn't even here! You have been mortally wounded while protecting a decoy!

Your dream of becoming a Musketeer came true surprisingly fast— and today it ends surprisingly soon.

THE END

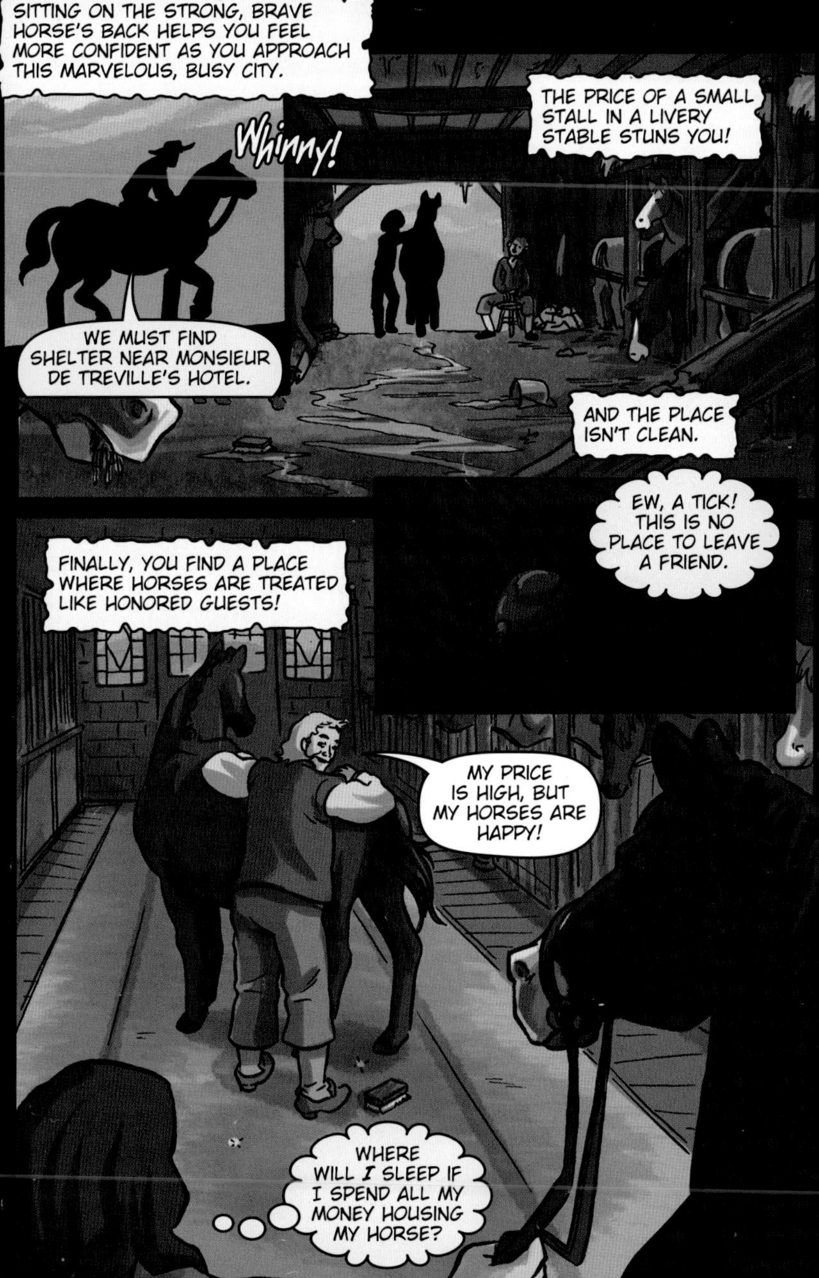
SITTING ON THE STRONG, BRAVE HORSE'S BACK HELPS YOU FEEL MORE CONFIDENT AS YOU APPROACH THIS MARVELOUS, BUSY CITY.
Whinny!
WE MUST FIND SHELTER NEAR MONSIEUR DE TREVILLE'S HOTEL.
THE PRICE OF A SMALL STALL IN A LIVERY STABLE STUNS YOU!
AND THE PLACE ISN'T CLEAN.
EW, A TICK! THIS IS NO PLACE TO LEAVE A FRIEND.
FINALLY, YOU FIND A PLACE WHERE HORSES ARE TREATED LIKE HONORED GUESTS!
MY PRICE IS HIGH, BUT MY HORSES ARE HAPPY!
WHERE WILL *I* SLEEP IF I SPEND ALL MY MONEY HOUSING MY HORSE?

GO ON TO THE NEXT PAGE.

WILL YOU . . .

. . . sneak back into the stable after dark to sleep
in the stall with Pinky?
TURN TO PAGE 39.

. . . ask Spurs the stable owner if you can work for
part of Pinky's boarding fee?
TURN TO PAGE 17.

You stay on the farm and return the sword to its hiding place beneath the floorboards. You often wonder if you missed something by not challenging yourself to do the "impossible." Over the years, you resent the simplicity of your life. You feel like a sleepwalker. You become careless.

One morning during your seventeenth year, while mucking out the barn, you neglect the most basic rules of safety. Instead of standing where the giant plow horse, Pinky, can see you or humming to alert him to your presence, you are lost in gloomy thoughts of missed glory.

A fly bites Pinky's flank, and the horse kicks you in the head! Just before your vision goes black, you feel strangely amused. You turned your back on danger, but in this seemingly safe place, danger has found *you*.

THE END

You beg for forgiveness. You were only trying to study the beauty of the stars.

You are let go with a warning. You continue to help Galileo, but you both learn to discuss science only with other like-minded scholars. Eventually, Galileo's "theory" is proven to be true. But by then, you and Galileo and Pinky are long gone from this world.

In your many years of studying the stars, you only rarely regret giving up your dream of becoming a Musketeer. The stars give you a sense of something larger and more lasting than the wars and changing politics of a soldier's life.

Still, you sometimes wonder what it would have been like to share a victory with brave men like Porthos, Aramis, Athos, and D'Artagnan and to shout, "All for one and one for all!"

THE END

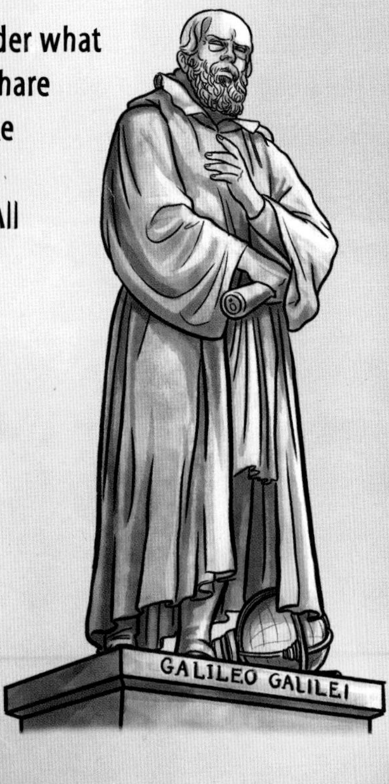
GALILEO GALILEI

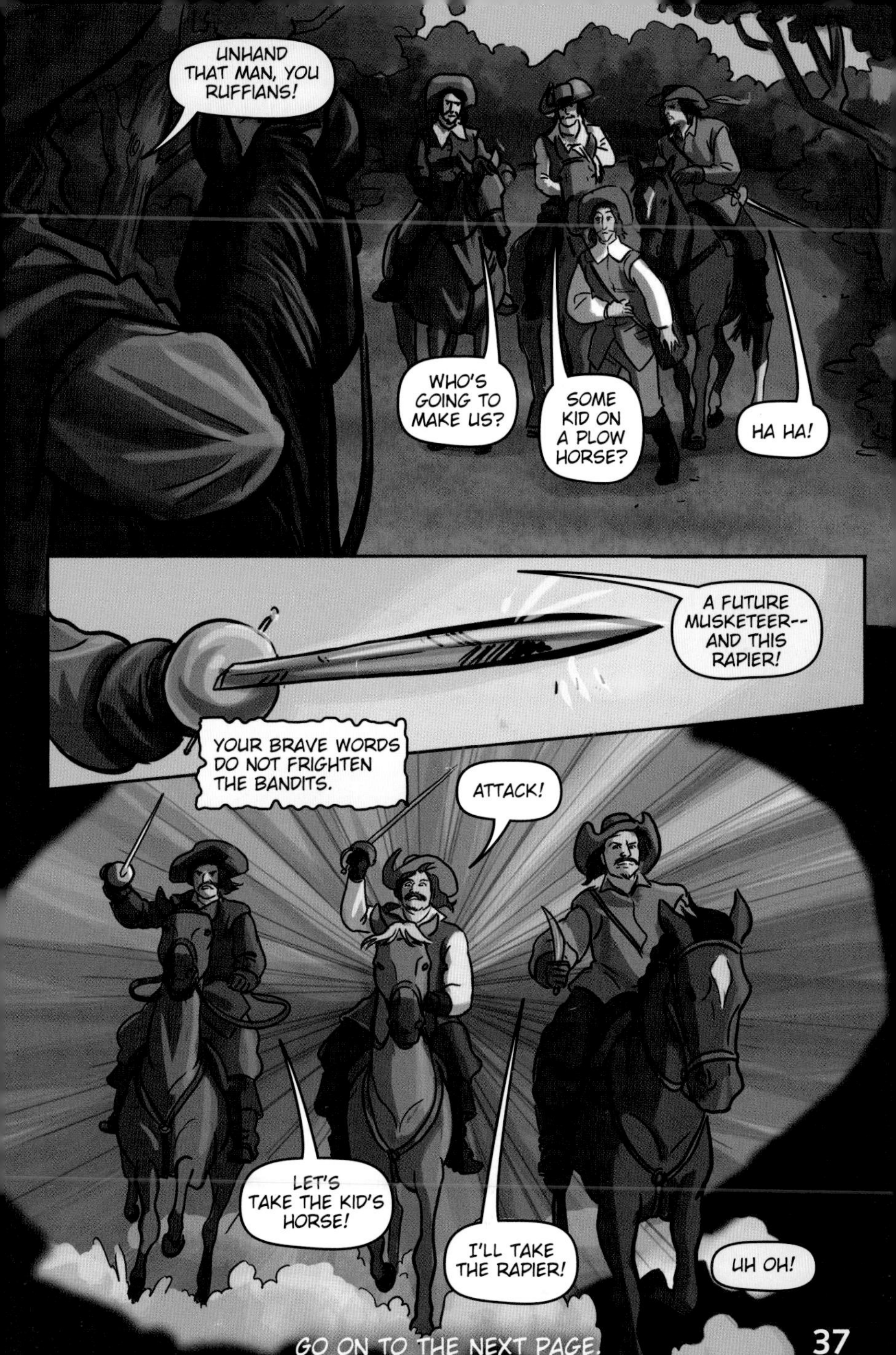
UNHAND THAT MAN, YOU RUFFIANS!
WHO'S GOING TO MAKE US?
SOME KID ON A PLOW HORSE?
HA HA!
A FUTURE MUSKETEER-- AND THIS RAPIER!
YOUR BRAVE WORDS DO NOT FRIGHTEN THE BANDITS.
ATTACK!
LET'S TAKE THE KID'S HORSE!
I'LL TAKE THE RAPIER!
UH OH!

GO ON TO THE NEXT PAGE.

Three seasoned warriors prove more than you can handle. Your sword arm is seriously wounded, and your rapier falls! You are soon dizzy from blood loss.

Before you fall, someone jumps up behind you. Strong arms hold you upright, and garlicky breath shouts near your ear, "Hy-ah! Go!" Then your vision goes blank.

You wake in a nearby inn with your wound neatly bandaged. A garlic-scented voice reports, "The child is coming around!"

Giles Poirier, a physician's assistant, explains to you that he dresses poorly while traveling to discourage bandits. Unfortunately, his clothing did not discourage those three.

Your arm was cut nearly to the bone! But thanks to the doctor's skill, you will be able to fight again.

During your long recovery, Giles and the doctor tell amazing stories of the lives they have saved and experiments they perform to advance the science of medicine.

38

TURN TO PAGE 55.

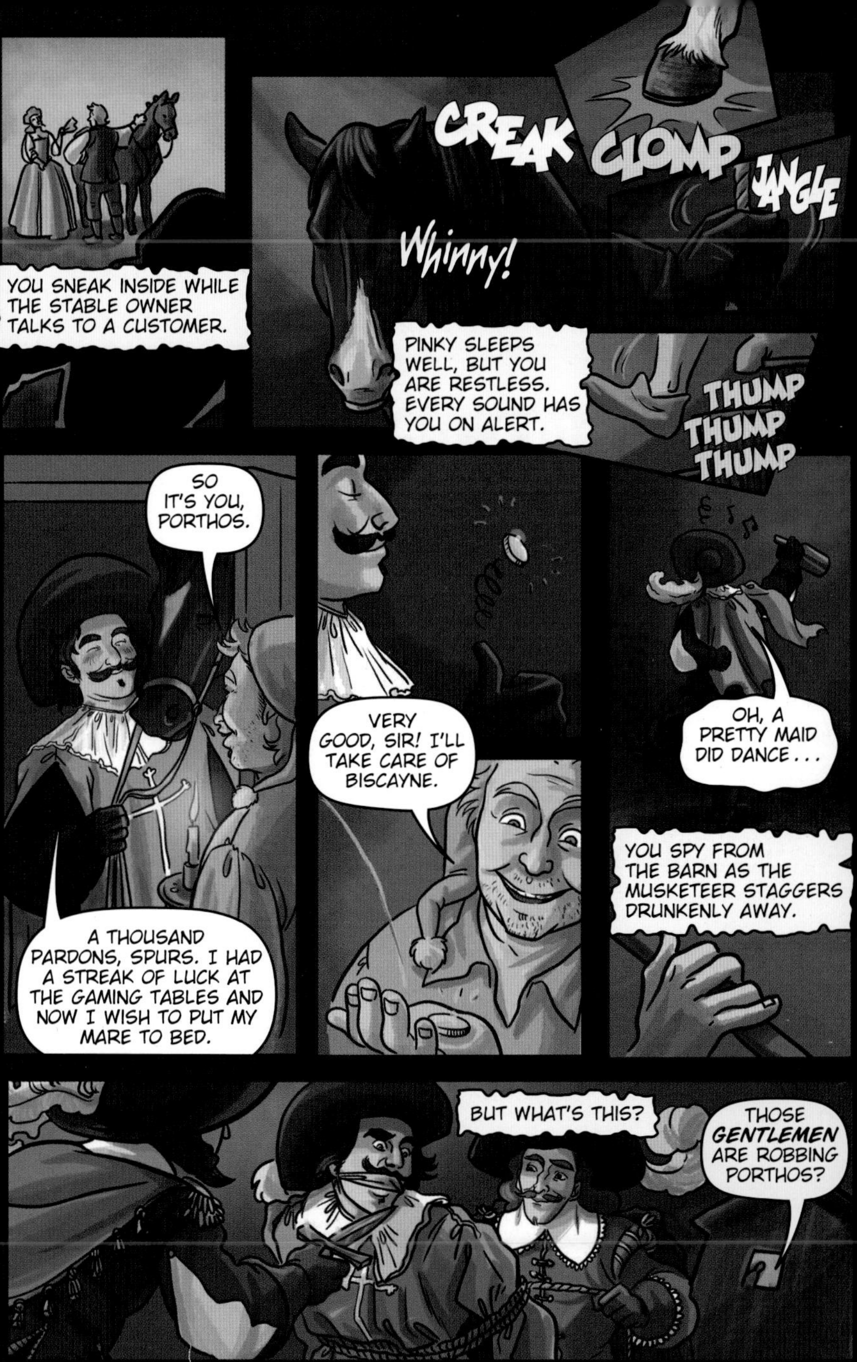
YOU SNEAK INSIDE WHILE THE STABLE OWNER TALKS TO A CUSTOMER.
CREAK
CLOMP
JANGLE
Whinny!
PINKY SLEEPS WELL, BUT YOU ARE RESTLESS. EVERY SOUND HAS YOU ON ALERT.
THUMP THUMP THUMP
SO IT'S YOU, PORTHOS.
A THOUSAND PARDONS, SPURS. I HAD A STREAK OF LUCK AT THE GAMING TABLES AND NOW I WISH TO PUT MY MARE TO BED.
VERY GOOD, SIR! I'LL TAKE CARE OF BISCAYNE.
OH, A PRETTY MAID DID DANCE . . .
YOU SPY FROM THE BARN AS THE MUSKETEER STAGGERS DRUNKENLY AWAY.
BUT WHAT'S THIS?
THOSE *GENTLEMEN* ARE ROBBING PORTHOS?

GO ON TO THE NEXT PAGE.

WILL YOU . . .

. . . shout at the top of your lungs to arouse the
whole neighborhood?
TURN TO PAGE 84.

. . . sneak up on the nearest one with
your rapier drawn?
TURN TO PAGE 43.

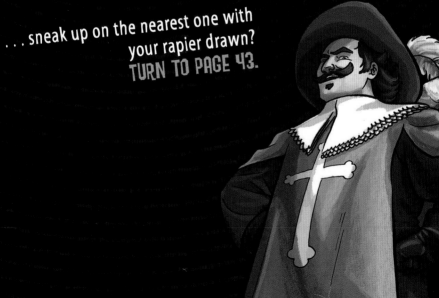

Under Richelieu's influence you gain in riches and cunning. Your money buys friendships with Musketeers. It also helps you break the weakest link in the chain binding the four inseparables.

Porthos, who is fond of gambling and wine, loses a fortune. You rescue him from his debt with Richelieu's money. Then you fill him with wine to discover the secrets he knows about the Queen.

With information about the Queen's misbehavior, Richelieu drives a wedge between her and the King. You tell yourself it's all for the good of France. But guilt rots your heart—and your arteries.

When you pass on to the next world at a young age, you leave your fortune to Treville's company. The money helps other Musketeers do a better job of upholding the troop's ideals.

Your fortune buys armor, weapons, uniforms, and other supplies for worthy young heroes. These brave men include your name when they lift their glasses to toast, "All for one and one for all!"

THE END

The light box was tempting, but you decide to keep drawing on your own. Your progress is slow, until finally the blank page begins to open to you, and your hands get better and better at drawing whatever you see or imagine.

This success comes alongside other successes with your Musketeer training. You get used to pushing past any difficulties.

Soon you are drawing, speaking Italian, and even bowing like a proper courtier, along with improving your swordsmanship, horseback riding, and other skills. Your family is proud of all you've learned, and on your eighteenth birthday, in 1627, Father declares that you are ready to go to Paris to become a Musketeer!

TURN TO PAGE 25.

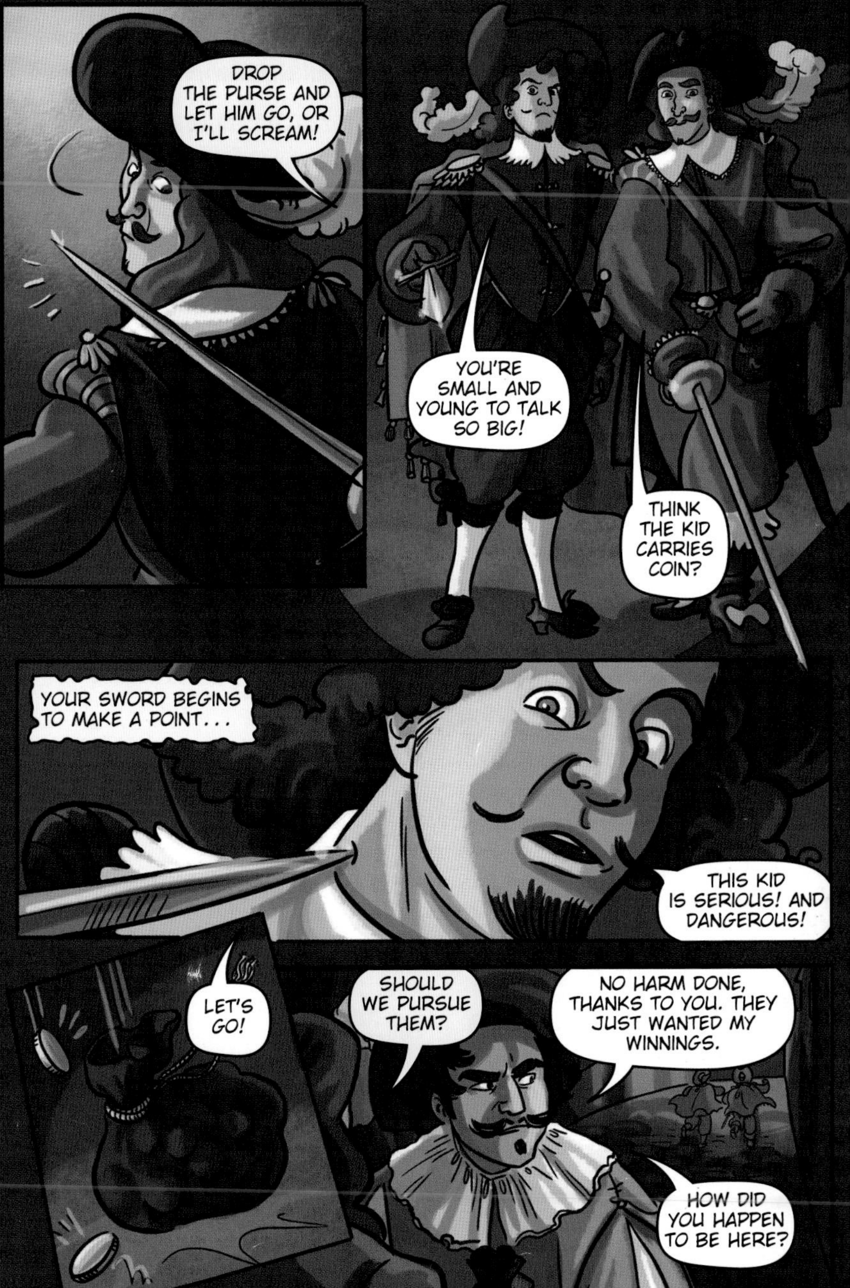
DROP THE PURSE AND LET HIM GO, OR I'LL SCREAM!
YOU'RE SMALL AND YOUNG TO TALK SO BIG!
THINK THE KID CARRIES COIN?
YOUR SWORD BEGINS TO MAKE A POINT...
THIS KID IS SERIOUS! AND DANGEROUS!
LET'S GO!
SHOULD WE PURSUE THEM?
NO HARM DONE, THANKS TO YOU. THEY JUST WANTED MY WINNINGS.
HOW DID YOU HAPPEN TO BE HERE?

GO ON TO THE NEXT PAGE.

You wonder if you should fib or tell the embarrassing truth. When you choose the truth, Porthos laughs and claps you on the back so hard, you almost fall over. "Your empty purse kept mine full," he says, "so you must allow me to reward you."

He pulls out several large coins and presses them into your hand. "Furthermore, I will escort you to see Monsieur de Treville tomorrow. I'll tell him that, even though you are young and small, you are not short on courage!"

Between Porthos's praise and Father's letter, Treville is impressed. "I cannot admit you directly into the Musketeers," he tells you the next morning, "but I can place you in the army of a nobleman who plans to free some princes being held captive by Spain. You can gain enough battle experience to become a Musketeer."

Your heart pounds with excitement.

44

TURN TO PAGE 48.

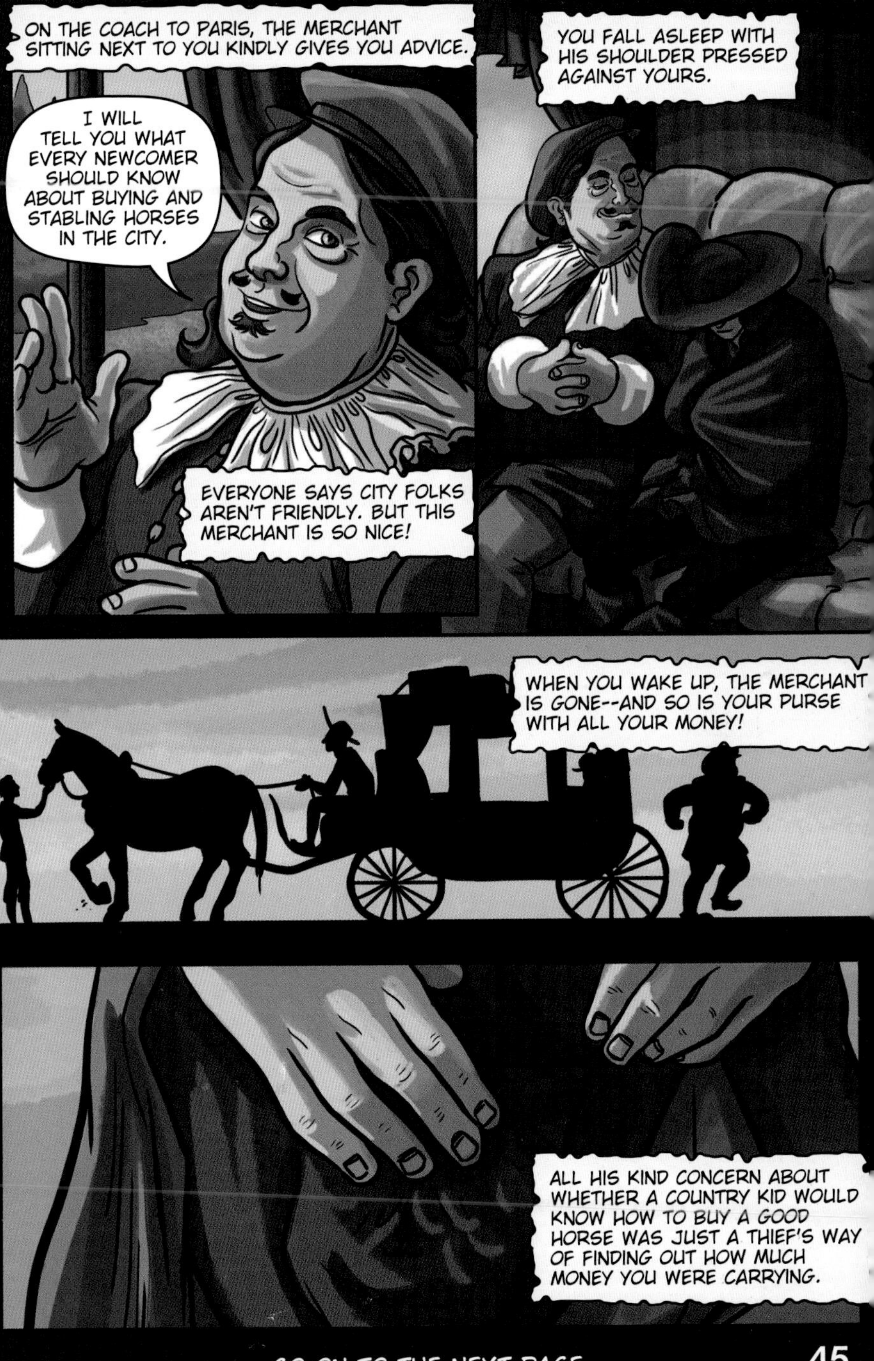
ON THE COACH TO PARIS, THE MERCHANT SITTING NEXT TO YOU KINDLY GIVES YOU ADVICE.
I WILL TELL YOU WHAT EVERY NEWCOMER SHOULD KNOW ABOUT BUYING AND STABLING HORSES IN THE CITY.
EVERYONE SAYS CITY FOLKS AREN'T FRIENDLY. BUT THIS MERCHANT IS SO NICE!
YOU FALL ASLEEP WITH HIS SHOULDER PRESSED AGAINST YOURS.
WHEN YOU WAKE UP, THE MERCHANT IS GONE--AND SO IS YOUR PURSE WITH ALL YOUR MONEY!
ALL HIS KIND CONCERN ABOUT WHETHER A COUNTRY KID WOULD KNOW HOW TO BUY A GOOD HORSE WAS JUST A THIEF'S WAY OF FINDING OUT HOW MUCH MONEY YOU WERE CARRYING.

GO ON TO THE NEXT PAGE.

WILL YOU . . .

. . . continue on to Paris even though you
are penniless?
TURN TO PAGE 59.

. . . make your way home?
TURN TO PAGE 27.

Being in the duke's army has given you a good taste of what it's like to have to follow orders every day. Frankly, the thought of traveling with a friend sharing adventures seems a lot more appealing. So instead of returning to the duke's army and trying to gain a place in the Musketeers, you and Giles set off on your own.

In your long career together, you fight many phony monsters and deceitful sorcerers. On many occasions, your Musketeer training saves your lives. When you grow too old to hold a sword with confidence, you return to a small farm where you write your memoirs.

Most people don't believe your amazing adventures. But you and Giles know that the truth is even more magical than fiction.

THE END

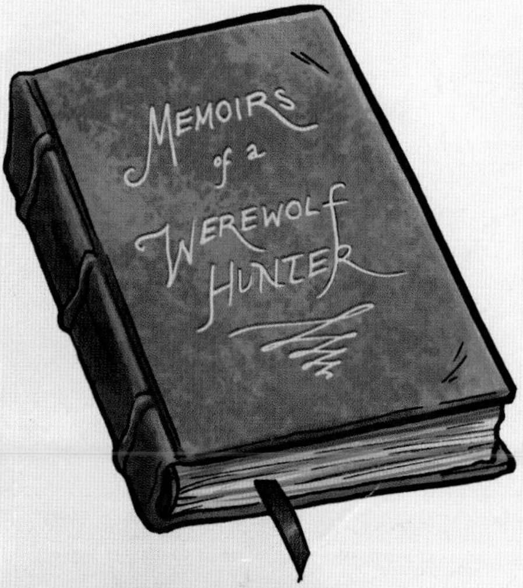
Memoirs of a Werewolf Hunter

Within weeks, you and Pinky leave Paris with a small troop of soldiers. You don't know what to think of the religious arguments between the Catholics and the Huguenots. After all, they both say they worship the same Prince of Peace.

Like many people from the Gascogne region, your family was originally Huguenot. When Louis XIII's father, good King Henry IV, converted to Catholicism in 1593 after the siege of Paris, your family went along with the change. All the people in your village did. But that was years before you were born.

The night before your first battle, fear torments you. The seasoned soldiers play cards, drink wine, laugh loudly, or stare gloomily into space. Are they as afraid as you are? You need battle experience to become a Musketeer. Will this horrible feeling pass once you survive your first day?

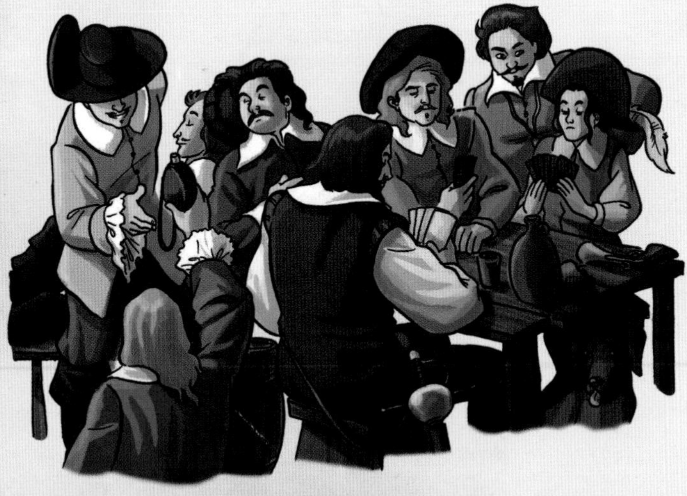

GO ON TO THE NEXT PAGE.

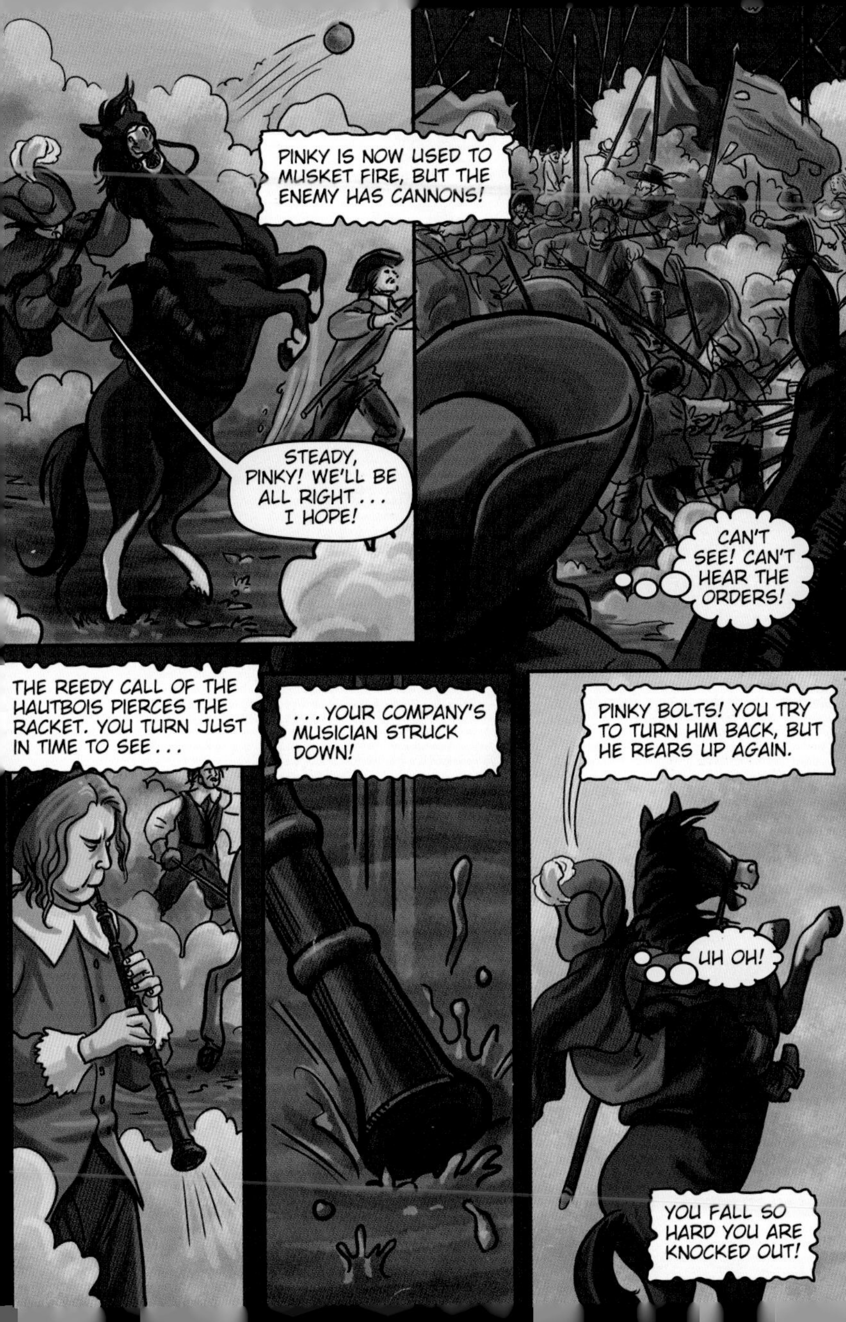
PINKY IS NOW USED TO MUSKET FIRE, BUT THE ENEMY HAS CANNONS!
STEADY, PINKY! WE'LL BE ALL RIGHT . . . I HOPE!
CAN'T SEE! CAN'T HEAR THE ORDERS!
THE REEDY CALL OF THE HAUTBOIS PIERCES THE RACKET. YOU TURN JUST IN TIME TO SEE . . .
. . . YOUR COMPANY'S MUSICIAN STRUCK DOWN!
PINKY BOLTS! YOU TRY TO TURN HIM BACK, BUT HE REARS UP AGAIN.
UH OH!
YOU FALL SO HARD YOU ARE KNOCKED OUT!

You don't like the sound of muskets any more than Pinky did. Forcing a horse to hold steady while you fire between its ears seems cruel.

For the first time since finding the rapier, you question your ambition to become a Musketeer. Truth be told, you feel homesick! Maybe Pinky isn't the only one who belongs on a farm.

When you whisper to Pinky, "Would you like to go home?" he snorts in agreement. You arrive in time for the plum harvest. The farm is so beautiful and quiet. And after the stench of the city, the air smells sweet.

Your parents are grateful to have your help at harvest. Pinky is as happy as a horse can be. You are surprised that you don't regret your decision. In the years to come, you decide you are glad that you went to Paris—and glad you came home!

THE END

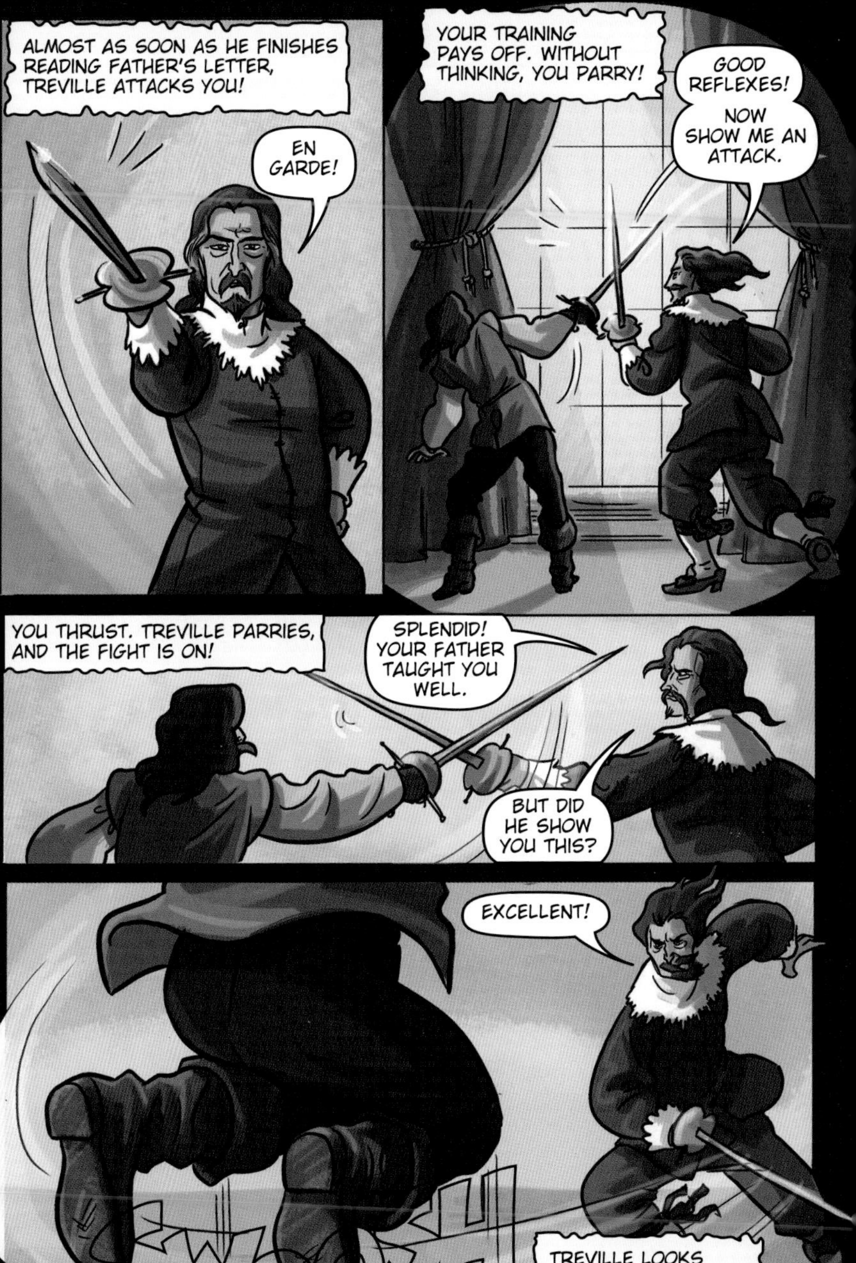
ALMOST AS SOON AS HE FINISHES READING FATHER'S LETTER, TREVILLE ATTACKS YOU!
EN GARDE!
YOUR TRAINING PAYS OFF. WITHOUT THINKING, YOU PARRY!
GOOD REFLEXES!
NOW SHOW ME AN ATTACK.
YOU THRUST. TREVILLE PARRIES, AND THE FIGHT IS ON!
SPLENDID! YOUR FATHER TAUGHT YOU WELL.
BUT DID HE SHOW YOU THIS?
EXCELLENT!
SWOOSH
TREVILLE LOOKS OLDER THAN FATHER, BUT HE'S SO QUICK!

GO ON TO THE NEXT PAGE.

Soon you are panting like a sheepdog in summer. You can't believe this old man is pushing you to the limit of your abilities. Then you get a lucky break. Treville trips on a lump in the carpet, and your rapier taps his chest.

Treville puts down his weapon to shake your hand. "Most impressive! Now let's go to the firing range to see what you can do with a musket."

Your face falls. Before you can say anything, Treville stops himself. "My mistake. Growing up on a farm, you have probably never even *seen* a musket."

You sigh with relief, adding quickly, "But I'm sure I can learn to shoot!"

Now Treville sighs. "I'm sure you can, but that will take time."

TURN TO PAGE 80.

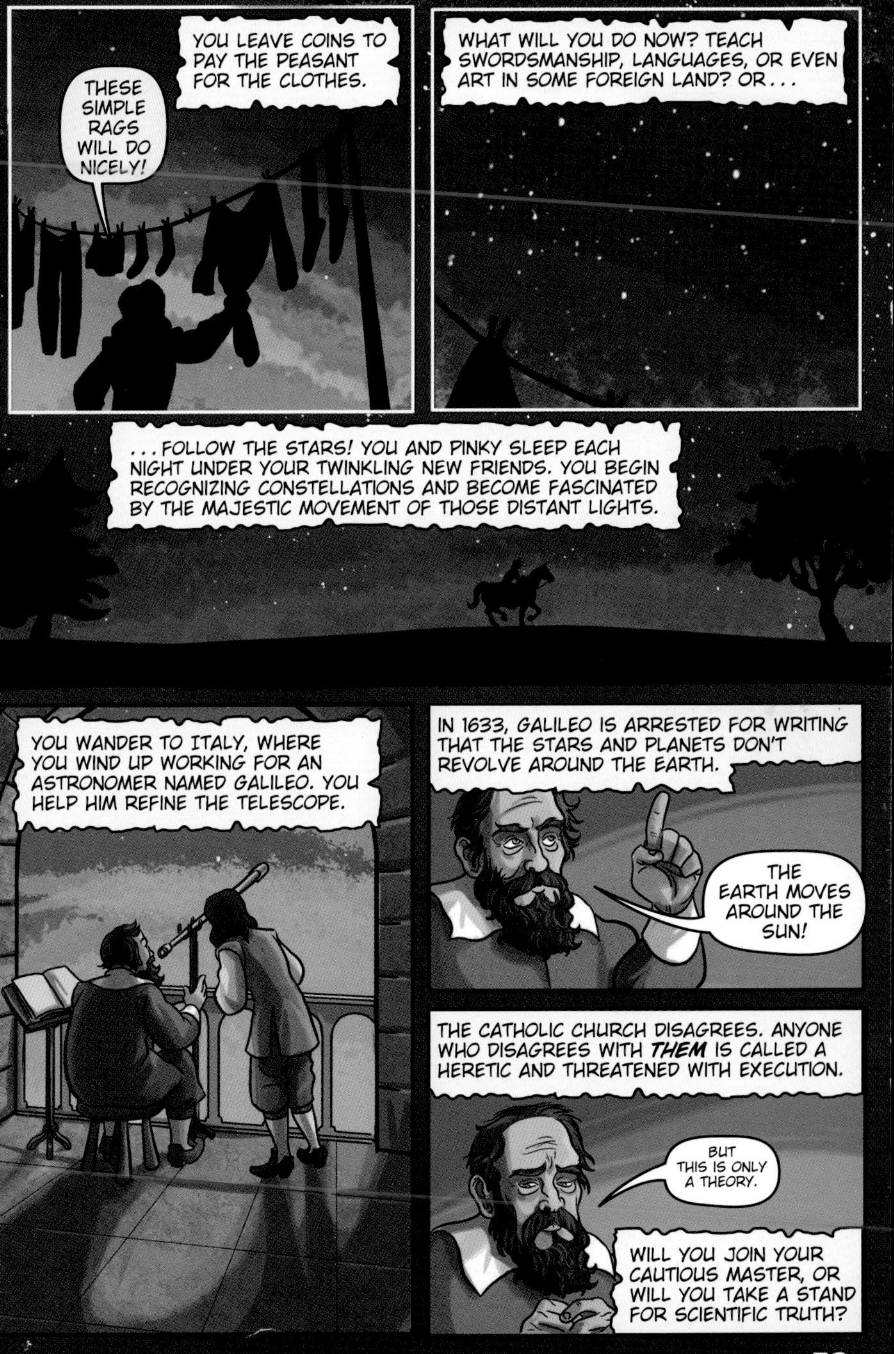
YOU LEAVE COINS TO PAY THE PEASANT FOR THE CLOTHES.
THESE SIMPLE RAGS WILL DO NICELY!
WHAT WILL YOU DO NOW? TEACH SWORDSMANSHIP, LANGUAGES, OR EVEN ART IN SOME FOREIGN LAND? OR . . .
. . . FOLLOW THE STARS! YOU AND PINKY SLEEP EACH NIGHT UNDER YOUR TWINKLING NEW FRIENDS. YOU BEGIN RECOGNIZING CONSTELLATIONS AND BECOME FASCINATED BY THE MAJESTIC MOVEMENT OF THOSE DISTANT LIGHTS.
YOU WANDER TO ITALY, WHERE YOU WIND UP WORKING FOR AN ASTRONOMER NAMED GALILEO. YOU HELP HIM REFINE THE TELESCOPE.
IN 1633, GALILEO IS ARRESTED FOR WRITING THAT THE STARS AND PLANETS DON'T REVOLVE AROUND THE EARTH.
THE EARTH MOVES AROUND THE SUN!
THE CATHOLIC CHURCH DISAGREES. ANYONE WHO DISAGREES WITH ***THEM*** IS CALLED A HERETIC AND THREATENED WITH EXECUTION.
BUT THIS IS ONLY A THEORY.
WILL YOU JOIN YOUR CAUTIOUS MASTER, OR WILL YOU TAKE A STAND FOR SCIENTIFIC TRUTH?

GO ON TO THE NEXT PAGE.

You are accused of helping a heretic!

WILL YOU . . .

. . . declare Galileo's brilliant discoveries
mere theories?
TURN TO PAGE 36.

. . . stand up for the truth?
TURN TO PAGE 79.

The doctor observes, "You seem smart and capable. I could use another assistant."

For the first time since finding the rapier, you question becoming a Musketeer. Being a healer is not as glorious as being a soldier. But there are different kinds of heroes. To the doctor's delight, you say, "Yes."

Because the roads you, Giles, and the doctor travel are dangerous, your training is not wasted. But you use the surgeon's knife much more than the sword.

When the doctor retires, you take his place. Countless people benefit from your efforts, including several wounded Musketeers. At one time their talk of duels and battles would have filled you with envy. Instead, you are disgusted by war's cruel waste.

At the end of your life, your only regret is that you never did find a cure for Giles' garlic breath, although your attempts led to several useful mouthwashes.

THE END

WILL YOU . . .

. . . give him a slap across the face with your glove, the call to a duel?

TURN TO PAGE 61.

. . . keep riding and ignore an insult, even to your honor?

TURN TO PAGE 109.

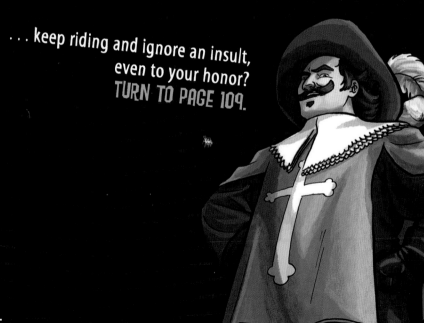

You wake up cold and stiff under a starry sky. Pinky's fuzzy lips nuzzle you, and you understand that the horse is sorry he hurt you. But you also understand that Pinky had good reasons for running.

You look around the battlefield. You shudder, realizing that you were left with the fallen soldiers waiting for burial. But you also realize that this means you are free. You do not have to keep fighting.

You cannot believe that you are thinking of running away after only one battle. But war did not turn out to be the glorious game you imagined. War is more mud than glory. Do you really want to stay a soldier?

You look up at the stars, hoping for a sign. They are incredibly beautiful, but they give no answer. You must make up your own mind.

GO ON TO THE NEXT PAGE.

WILL YOU . . .

. . . search for your company and ask to be sent back to Paris?
TURN TO PAGE 64.

. . . leave the army without permission?
TURN TO PAGE 53.

Although you hate to start out by asking for a favor, Treville won't let the child of his onetime rescuer starve.

Luckily, a local duchess needs people for her guard. On Treville's recommendation, she provides you with room, board, and the use of a horse while on duty. She also gives you a small salary, from which she deducts the cost of your uniform and weapon. To earn this, you help protect her large estates.

Up until now, you have only read about such riches. Even the duchess's maid wears finer clothes than you have ever seen! Yet the peasants who work her lands can barely feed their children. When your duties demand that you shoot rebellious peasants, you desert!

GO ON TO THE NEXT PAGE.

For weeks, you live in the woods. You never before questioned the fact that some people are dukes while others are peasants. But what good are dukes—or kings—who do not take care of their people?

One night you are so lonely you go to a small tavern. The tavern keeper accepts your offer to wash dishes in exchange for a meal. You overhear people talking about revolution! It stirs your blood. You join the cause!

You become a printer's apprentice, risking your life to hand out pamphlets about freedom and the overthrowing of selfish kings. You are embarrassed when you think about your former plans to defend the King as a Musketeer.

You do not live long enough to see the French Revolution begin in 1789. In time, France will be known as the land of Liberty, Equality, and Fraternity. For you these words would have been even sweeter than the Musketeer cheer of "All for one and one for all!"

THE END

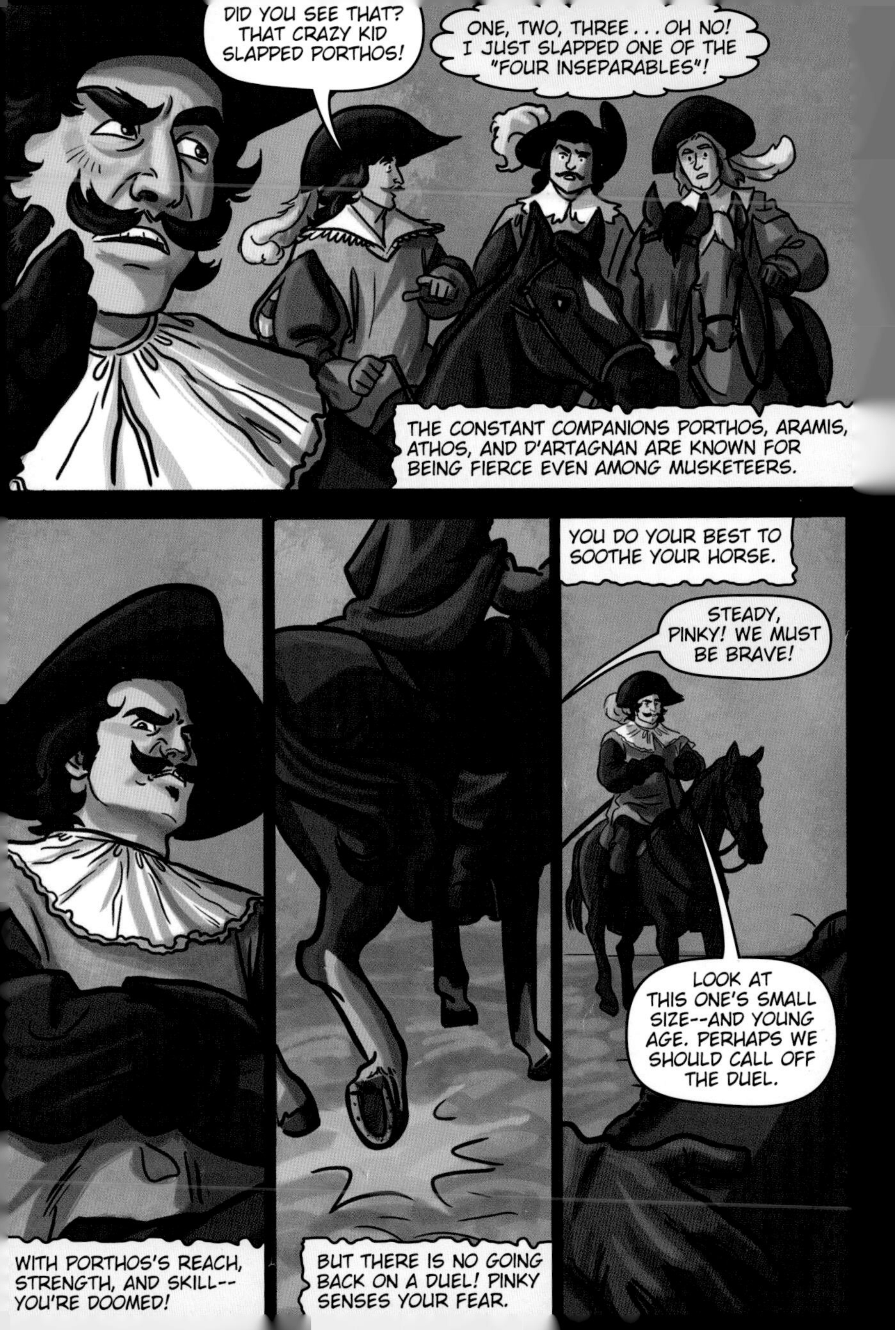
DID YOU SEE THAT? THAT CRAZY KID SLAPPED PORTHOS!
ONE, TWO, THREE . . . OH NO! I JUST SLAPPED ONE OF THE "FOUR INSEPARABLES"!
THE CONSTANT COMPANIONS PORTHOS, ARAMIS, ATHOS, AND D'ARTAGNAN ARE KNOWN FOR BEING FIERCE EVEN AMONG MUSKETEERS.
WITH PORTHOS'S REACH, STRENGTH, AND SKILL-- YOU'RE DOOMED!
BUT THERE IS NO GOING BACK ON A DUEL! PINKY SENSES YOUR FEAR.
YOU DO YOUR BEST TO SOOTHE YOUR HORSE.
STEADY, PINKY! WE MUST BE BRAVE!
LOOK AT THIS ONE'S SMALL SIZE--AND YOUNG AGE. PERHAPS WE SHOULD CALL OFF THE DUEL.

Call off the duel? That would destroy your honor after only one day in Paris. And it offends your Gascon pride.

WILL YOU SUGGEST . . .

. . . a less deadly duel—a test of horsemanship?
TURN TO PAGE 92.

. . . a duel with dull practice swords, with Monsieur de Treville as judge?
TURN TO PAGE 78.

Jean-Pierre hops up around your waist, holding his ankles behind your back. The priest's belt helps secure your "belly" as you walk out of the dungeons to freedom!

You keep the disguise on until you reach Musketeer headquarters. The priest costume fools even the four inseparables, until you pull off the fake beard and Jean-Pierre steps out from under your robe. Everyone cheers!

Now you are genuinely welcomed as a Musketeer. The darkness that entered your heart when you deceived Father evaporates like dew on a hot day. You write him a letter telling all. You confess to Treville, who forgives you.

Over the next twenty years, you prove yourself to be an excellent Musketeer. Before you retire, you've become second in command under Captain D'Artagnan. Whenever new cadets ask your advice, you warn them not to take shortcuts in matters of conscience—for a Musketeer's word is even more valuable than his sword.

THE END

In the morning, you follow the trail to your company of soldiers. When you ask permission to return to Paris, your commander laughs! "We'd all like to leave. But we can't go home until the job is done."

You fight and fight, but the war never ends. The war was already nine years old when you joined in 1627. How much longer can it last?

Then one day, you fear the end is coming for *your* company. You are outnumbered, with no escape route.

The commander insists you must attack the castle at dawn. You beg him to wait until fortifications are built to protect your company from enemy fire as they approach the castle.

He says, "My orders are to attack at dawn."

Your comrades grumble, "If we can't disable their cannons, we're doomed!"

You have heard there is a way to do that with just a hammer and nails. If you dare to try it.

GO ON TO THE NEXT PAGE.

WILL YOU . . .

. . . sneak out of camp and try to disable the enemy's cannons?
TURN TO PAGE 70.

. . . trust the experienced commander to know what he's doing?
TURN TO PAGE 10.

The old woman introduces herself as an innocent herbalist. But from your medical conversations with Giles, you know that herbs can harm as well as cure. You are careful not to drink anything until you see her swallow something from the same pitcher.

But the inner surface of the goblet in which she serves your drink had already been coated with a strong but invisible potion!

Almost instantly you feel yourself changing from soldier to savage! Your fingers turn into claws. Your arms sprout fur. Your teeth grow into fangs!

The witch cackles. "Don't fight it. Be free! Go wild. You are a wolf!"

Some tiny part of your mind clings desperately to reason. People cannot change into wolves. Only fools and madmen believe such things!

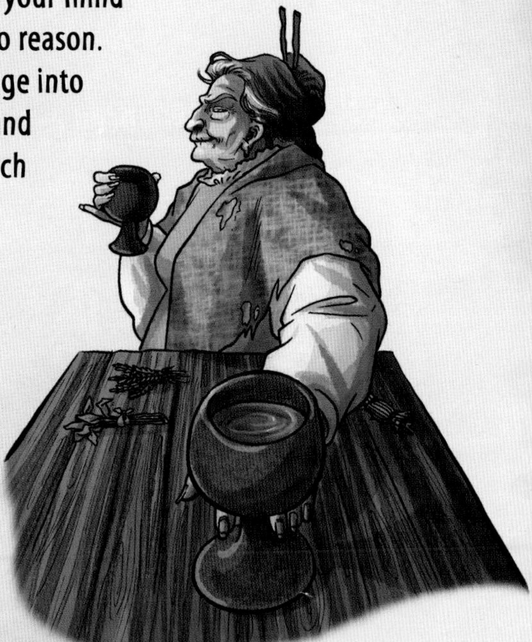

GO ON TO THE NEXT PAGE.

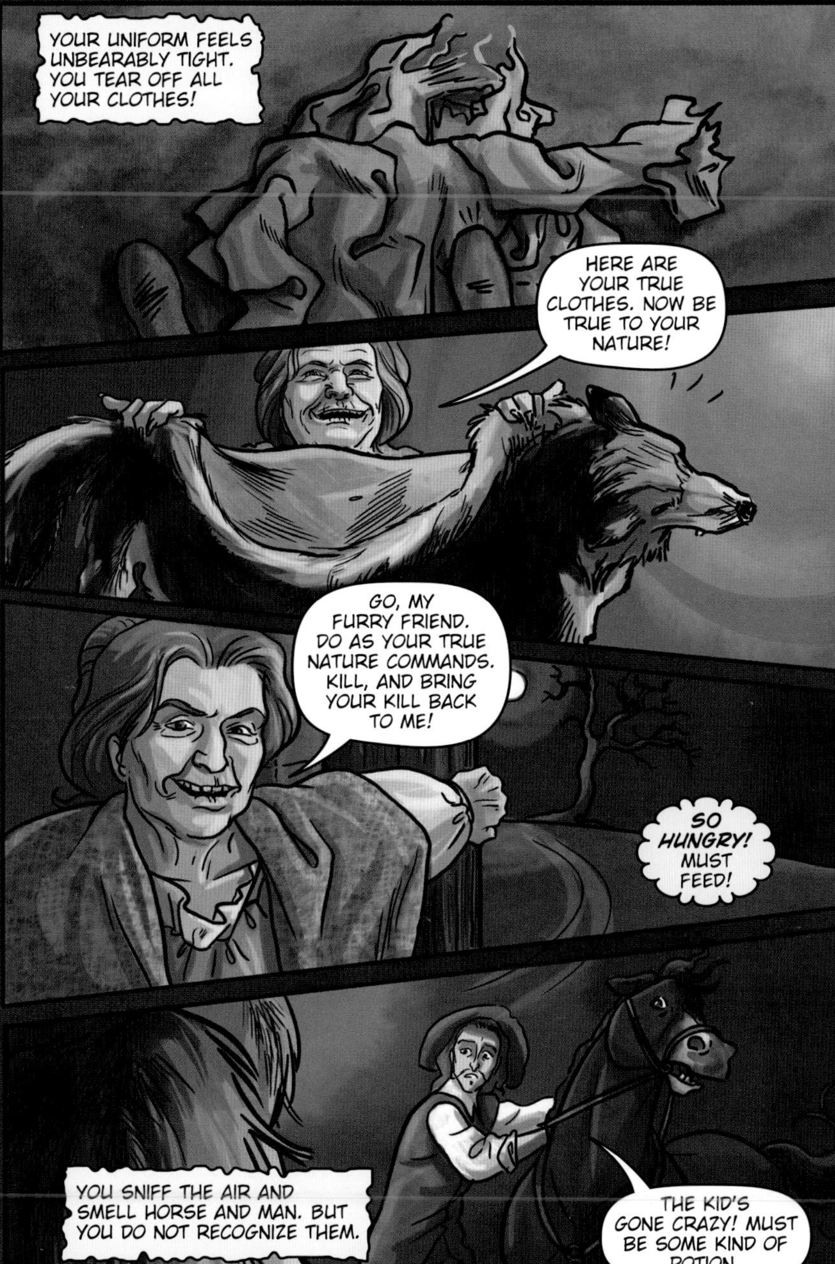
YOUR UNIFORM FEELS UNBEARABLY TIGHT. YOU TEAR OFF ALL YOUR CLOTHES!
HERE ARE YOUR TRUE CLOTHES. NOW BE TRUE TO YOUR NATURE!
GO, MY FURRY FRIEND. DO AS YOUR TRUE NATURE COMMANDS. KILL, AND BRING YOUR KILL BACK TO ME!
SO HUNGRY! MUST FEED!
YOU SNIFF THE AIR AND SMELL HORSE AND MAN. BUT YOU DO NOT RECOGNIZE THEM.
THE KID'S GONE CRAZY! MUST BE SOME KIND OF POTION.

TURN TO PAGE 82.

You return to Treville's hotel with a renewed sense of determination and peace. Whenever your Gascon temper tempts you to be rash, you think of the serene statue of the Madonna.

This prevents St. Pierre from getting your goat again. Frustrated by your calm lack of response, he eventually stops teasing you.

Treville sees your growing maturity and finds a place for you in a local nobleman's troop. If you prove yourself in battle, you may become a Musketeer!

Your first battle is a tax riot in a small village. The local nobleman, a marquis, will not put up with disturbances on his lands.

Your commander orders your troop to fire at the peasants. The peasants are armed only with pitchforks and rocks.

"Can't we negotiate with them?" you ask.

The commander laughs. "They need a good scare, not words."

GO ON TO THE NEXT PAGE.

WILL YOU . . .

. . . obey your commanding officer like a good
soldier should?

TURN TO PAGE 108.

. . . look for a peaceful solution?
TURN TO PAGE 98.

WITH MUD FOR MAKEUP, BORROWED DARK CLOTHING, A HAMMER, AND NAILS, YOU SNEAK TOWARD THE CASTLE. YOU THROW PEBBLES AND HOWL LIKE A WOLF PACK TO CONFUSE THE ENEMY GUARDS.

YOU MIRACULOUSLY MANAGE TO HAMMER NAILS INTO ALL THE CANNONS WITHOUT BEING DISCOVERED!

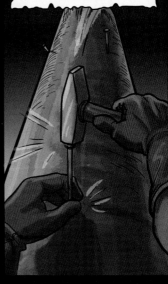

UNFORTUNATELY, AS YOU MAKE YOUR ESCAPE . . .

THERE'S ONE OF THOSE NOISY WOLVES!

BLAST

YOU NEVER MAKE IT BACK, BUT YOUR COURAGEOUS ACTION SAVES YOUR COMPANY. YOU REALLY WOULD HAVE MADE A GREAT MUSKETEER!

THAT STUBBORN KID SAVED US ALL!

The END

You reason it wouldn't be wrong to help find traitors. So while Jean-Pierre sleeps, you ask to meet with Richelieu, promising to uncover any Musketeer plots against him or the King. Outside those horrible walls, you are still not free. The cardinal's cold smile has wrapped around your heart like a snake.

At Musketeer headquarters, your "miraculous" release is greeted with suspicion. Even more than before your arrest, the company of Musketeers shies away from you. You can't blame them, since you *are* a spy!

Then one night you find out Jean-Pierre's execution has been scheduled for the next day! By pretending to be fast asleep in a tavern, you overhear the four inseparables planning a daring rescue. If the Musketeers successfully rescue Jean-Pierre from the gallows, Richelieu will surely blame you, his spy, for not warning him.

GO ON TO THE NEXT PAGE.

WILL YOU . . .

. . . rush to tell Richelieu?
TURN TO PAGE 31.

. . . flee France and Richelieu's revenge?
TURN TO PAGE 91.

The inspiration you felt in the church goes away when you meet the countess's mean children. When you draw them the way they really look, the countess is insulted. When you make them look like kindhearted saints, she does not recognize them.

You miss the excitement of training with the Musketeers. In your free moments, you join the courtiers who gather to watch their drills. Drawing sketches of the Musketeers gives you back your artistic inspiration. It also catches the King's attention!

King Louis XIII shows you his own sketchbooks. He commissions you to paint his favorite horse. You like this much better than drawing the countess's kids. A commission from the King makes you famous.

You travel to the capitals of Europe and mix with royalty and scholars. Your life is nothing like the one you imagined, but it is long and happy.

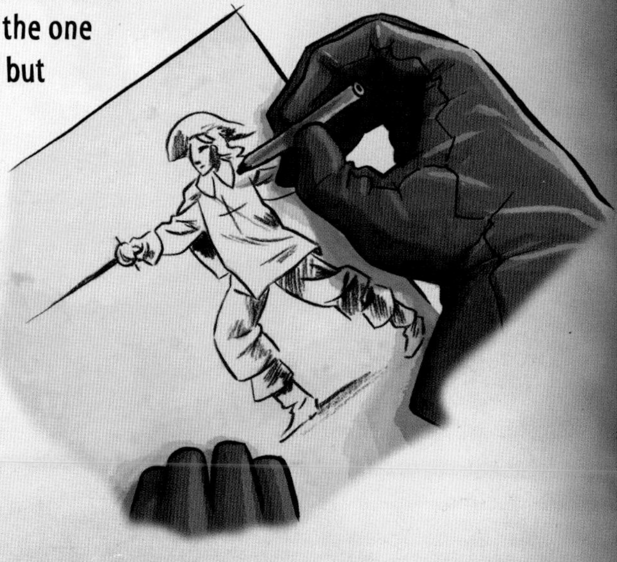

THE END

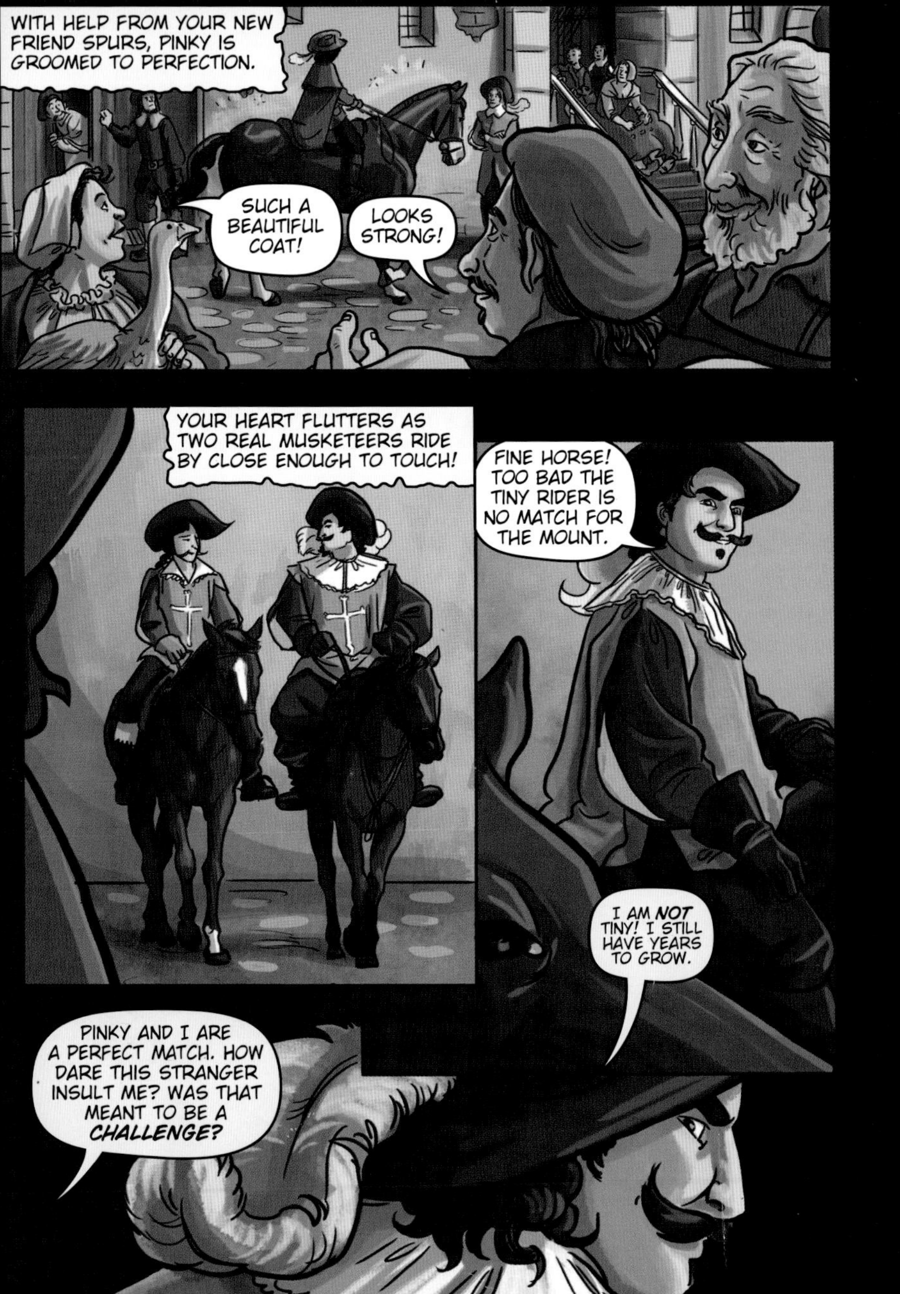
WITH HELP FROM YOUR NEW FRIEND SPURS, PINKY IS GROOMED TO PERFECTION.
SUCH A BEAUTIFUL COAT!
LOOKS STRONG!
YOUR HEART FLUTTERS AS TWO REAL MUSKETEERS RIDE BY CLOSE ENOUGH TO TOUCH!
FINE HORSE! TOO BAD THE TINY RIDER IS NO MATCH FOR THE MOUNT.
I AM *NOT* TINY! I STILL HAVE YEARS TO GROW.
PINKY AND I ARE A PERFECT MATCH. HOW DARE THIS STRANGER INSULT ME? WAS THAT MEANT TO BE A ***CHALLENGE?***

TURN TO PAGE 56.

St. Pierre has the money to bribe his way out of trouble. The cardinal threatens you with a trip to the terrible prison called the Bastille—or worse! Monsieur de Treville pleads with Richelieu, explaining that this is your first offense, and you are just a foolish youngster from the country.

Finally, Richelieu relents, on the condition that you leave Paris. The Musketeers are disgusted with you for forcing Treville to humble himself.

You go home in shame. You have, however, learned a valuable lesson. You never again let your anger overrule your judgment, nor are you ever tempted to take the "easy" route of being sneaky. These virtues help you build a good life, although you will never have a chance to prove you could have been a great Musketeer.

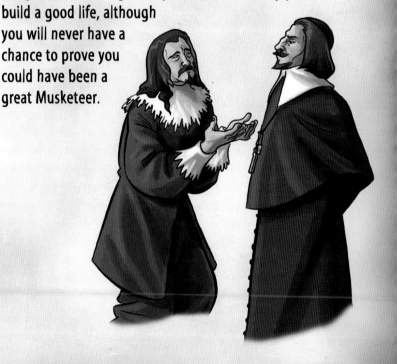

THE END

While Giles takes a look around with Pinky, you approach the witch's crude cabin in the woods. The door opens before you have a chance to knock. The old woman's face is wrinkled, but her eyes are quick with a fierce intelligence. She exclaims, "Such a fine soldier! To what do I owe this honor?"

You almost blurt out your mission. But you realize this might not be the wisest course. What if she really is behind the robberies?

GO ON TO THE NEXT PAGE.

WILL YOU . . .

. . . tell the witch that you are lost and seeking shelter for the night?
TURN TO PAGE 66.

. . . tell her you have heard that she is a powerful witch who has magical potions and you are here to buy?
TURN TO PAGE 9.

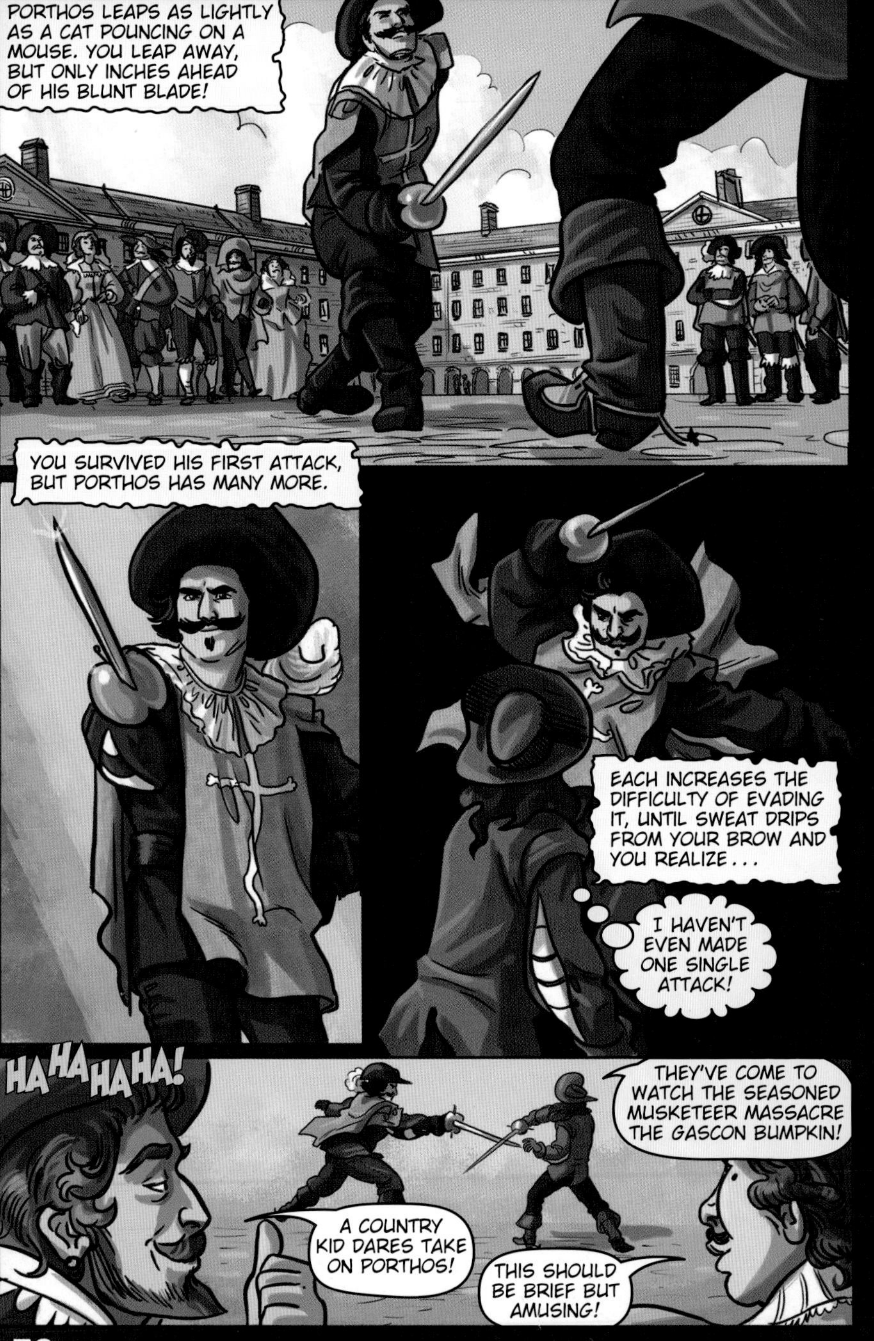
PORTHOS LEAPS AS LIGHTLY AS A CAT POUNCING ON A MOUSE. YOU LEAP AWAY, BUT ONLY INCHES AHEAD OF HIS BLUNT BLADE!
YOU SURVIVED HIS FIRST ATTACK, BUT PORTHOS HAS MANY MORE.
EACH INCREASES THE DIFFICULTY OF EVADING IT, UNTIL SWEAT DRIPS FROM YOUR BROW AND YOU REALIZE . . .
I HAVEN'T EVEN MADE ONE SINGLE ATTACK!
HAHAHAHA!
THEY'VE COME TO WATCH THE SEASONED MUSKETEER MASSACRE THE GASCON BUMPKIN!
A COUNTRY KID DARES TAKE ON PORTHOS!
THIS SHOULD BE BRIEF BUT AMUSING!

TURN TO PAGE 105.

You walked away from one war, but you refuse to be a coward again. You speak out for the truth. Your reward is to be sentenced to execution!

When you find out that you are to be burned alive, you wonder if you can change your testimony, but it is too late. This terrible execution is meant to be a lesson to everyone who witnesses it.

You face this as bravely as any Musketeer, standing up not for king and country but for reason and truth. You know someday you and Galileo will be proven correct—

—and you are right!

THE END

Captain de Treville is not kidding. There are thirty steps to loading and firing a musket! He leaves you to learn them and report to him again in a few days.

You struggle to hear your instructor over the thunderous noise of the powerful firearms as Musketeers practice around you. You feel as jumpy as a horse with a stall full of flies.

You take out pen and paper to write down the instructions. Next to each step, you make a quick sketch.

When Treville sees your Musket Manual, he slaps you on the back. "This is marvelous! You must make a copy for us to keep on the firing range."

Though you are not as quick as the experienced Musketeers, Treville is astounded by your progress. He arranges for you to gain some battle experience in the company of a country duke. You're one step closer to being a Musketeer!

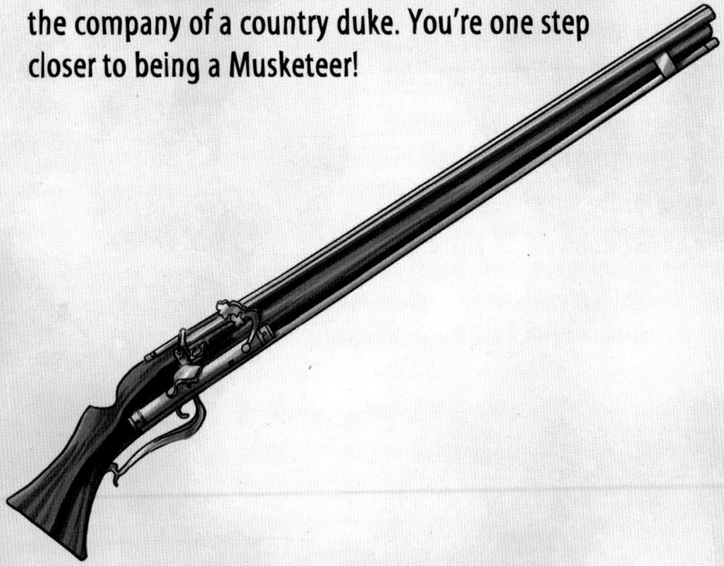

GO ON TO THE NEXT PAGE.

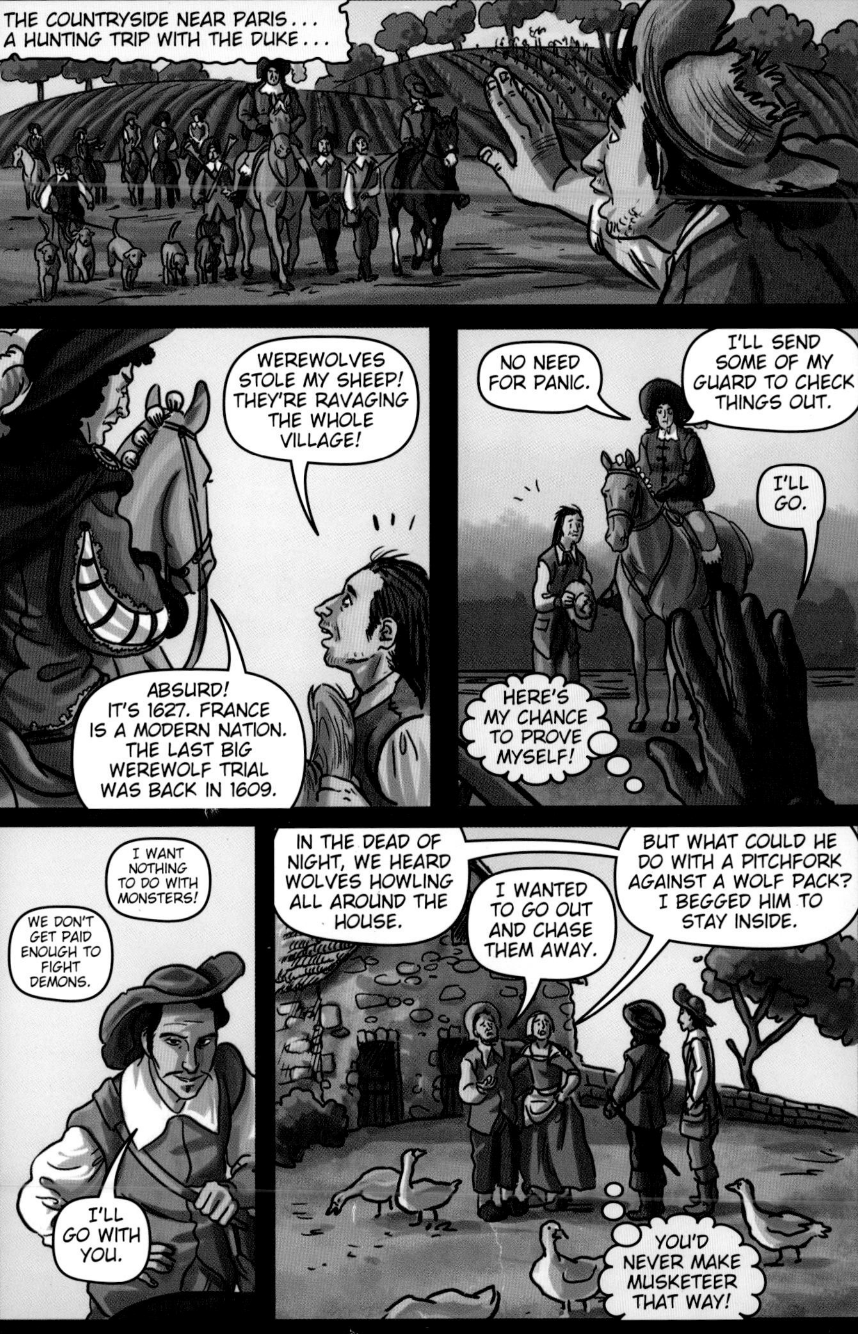
THE COUNTRYSIDE NEAR PARIS . . .
A HUNTING TRIP WITH THE DUKE . . .
WEREWOLVES STOLE MY SHEEP! THEY'RE RAVAGING THE WHOLE VILLAGE!
ABSURD! IT'S 1627. FRANCE IS A MODERN NATION. THE LAST BIG WEREWOLF TRIAL WAS BACK IN 1609.
NO NEED FOR PANIC.
I'LL SEND SOME OF MY GUARD TO CHECK THINGS OUT.
I'LL GO.
HERE'S MY CHANCE TO PROVE MYSELF!
I WANT NOTHING TO DO WITH MONSTERS!
WE DON'T GET PAID ENOUGH TO FIGHT DEMONS.
I'LL GO WITH YOU.
IN THE DEAD OF NIGHT, WE HEARD WOLVES HOWLING ALL AROUND THE HOUSE.
I WANTED TO GO OUT AND CHASE THEM AWAY.
BUT WHAT COULD HE DO WITH A PITCHFORK AGAINST A WOLF PACK? I BEGGED HIM TO STAY INSIDE.
YOU'D NEVER MAKE MUSKETEER THAT WAY!

TURN TO PAGE 94.

You lope toward the village, eager to sink your fangs into geese and sheep.

Suddenly, a rope falls over your shoulders!

Giles wraps you in his coat and fills your mouth with water. "Drink!" he commands. "The witch gave you a drug to make you *think* you are a werewolf."

The itchy feeling on your skin turns to sweat. Giles grins. "The poison is leaving you."

Giles' garlicky breath gives you the comfort of something familiar as he reports, "The witch's smokehouse is full of meat. Yet she raises no livestock. I also saw several wolf skins."

You struggle to understand Giles' theory. "I think . . . she drugs hungry vagrants and convinces them to steal for her."

It makes sense! If the witch's potion had such a powerful effect on you, what would it do to a half-starved person?

GO ON TO THE NEXT PAGE.

In the morning, when you feel fully human again,

WILL YOU . . .

. . . arrest the witch and bring her to the duke to face trial?
TURN TO PAGE 11.

. . . ride back for reinforcements so you have enough help to arrest her "wolf pack" too?
TURN TO PAGE 111.

Your shout wakes the neighbors and Spurs the stable owner. They rescue Porthos.

The fact that you sneaked into the stable makes Spurs distrust you. He returns your boarding fee and sends you away. Porthos is grateful for the rescue, but he is not impressed with your character or courage.

When you arrive at Treville's hotel, Porthos has already told the story. Treville reads Father's letter and agrees to let you train with him for a while, but only until you find a position in a less famous troop. You try to befriend the Musketeers, but gossip about your first night in Paris keeps you from gaining any friends.

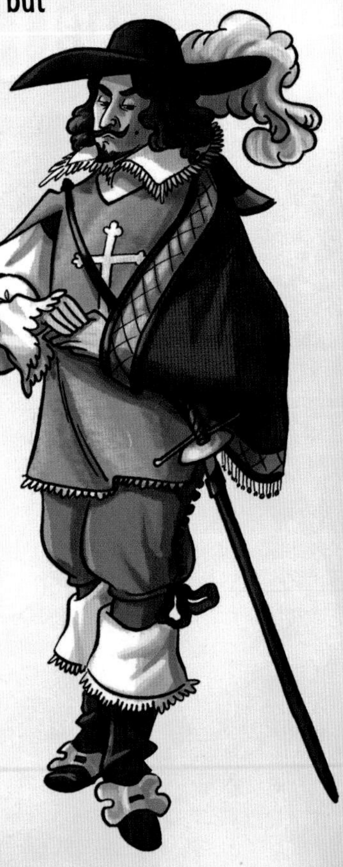

Your Gascon pride is hurt, especially the teasing you get from St. Pierre, a highborn Musketeer who sneers at your clothes and at Pinky's lack of breeding. He calls you a clumsy bumpkin!

Dueling is illegal, but many people risk it to prove their worth. You are tempted.

GO ON TO THE NEXT PAGE.

WILL YOU . . .

. . . suggest he put his sword behind his words and duel with you?
TURN TO PAGE 24.

. . . find some way to overcome your anger?
TURN TO PAGE 89.

You never imagined yourself becoming an artist for the church. But the work is satisfying. You move up from painting small pictures of saints to become the apprentice of a stained glass master.

Eventually, you become a master yourself. When the sun shines through your work, it looks divine!

You cannot go as far as becoming a priest yourself. But working near all their quiet prayers does soothe your Gascon temper. The peace inspired by the first sculpture you drew stays with you. You no longer feel the urge to fight.

When you look back on your goal to become a Musketeer, you feel relieved that it did not work out. After all, where would your soul go if you spent your whole life killing people in duels? It would be too much of a risk to find out! You live the rest of your life at peace.

THE END

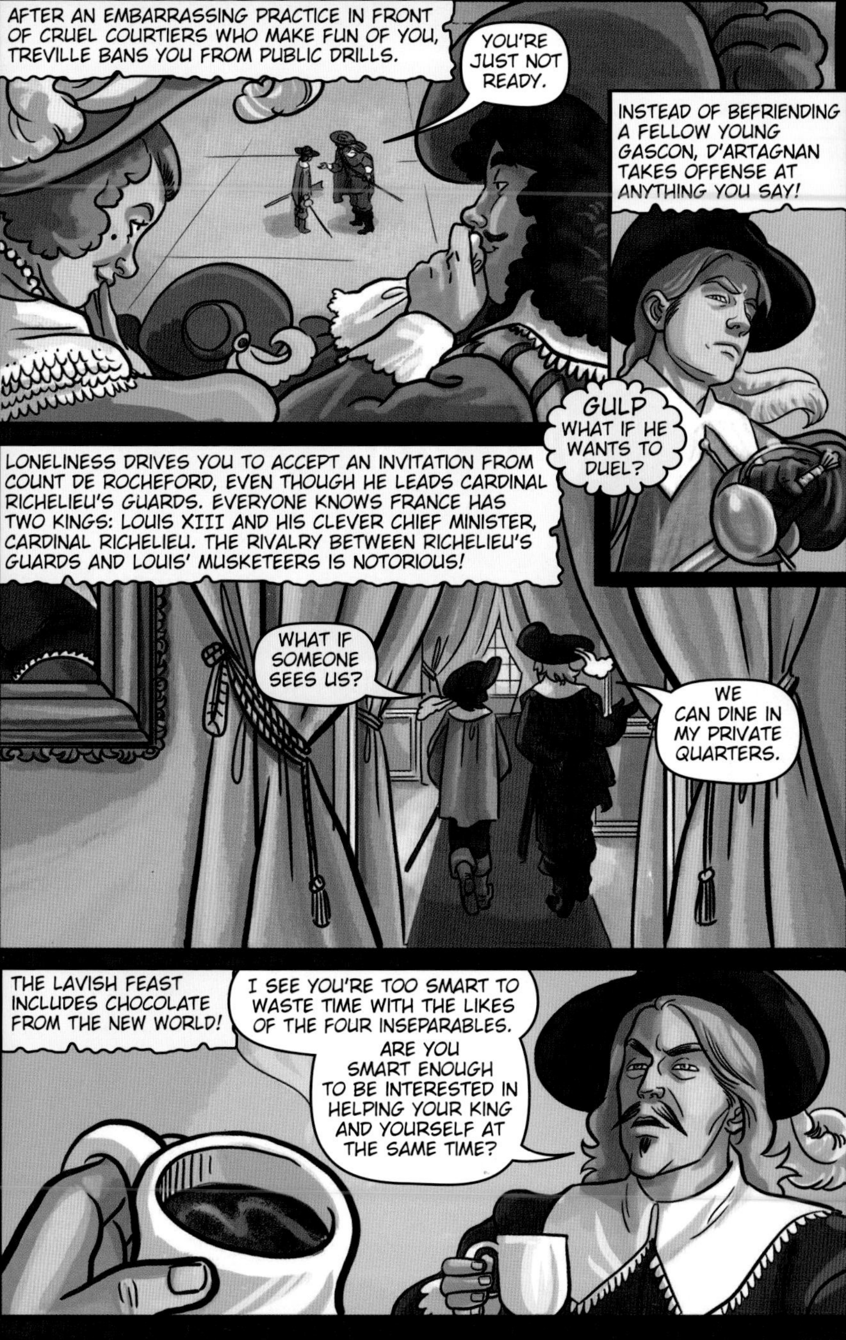
AFTER AN EMBARRASSING PRACTICE IN FRONT OF CRUEL COURTIERS WHO MAKE FUN OF YOU, TREVILLE BANS YOU FROM PUBLIC DRILLS.
YOU'RE JUST NOT READY.
INSTEAD OF BEFRIENDING A FELLOW YOUNG GASCON, D'ARTAGNAN TAKES OFFENSE AT ANYTHING YOU SAY!
GULP
WHAT IF HE WANTS TO DUEL?
LONELINESS DRIVES YOU TO ACCEPT AN INVITATION FROM COUNT DE ROCHEFORD, EVEN THOUGH HE LEADS CARDINAL RICHELIEU'S GUARDS. EVERYONE KNOWS FRANCE HAS TWO KINGS: LOUIS XIII AND HIS CLEVER CHIEF MINISTER, CARDINAL RICHELIEU. THE RIVALRY BETWEEN RICHELIEU'S GUARDS AND LOUIS' MUSKETEERS IS NOTORIOUS!
WHAT IF SOMEONE SEES US?
WE CAN DINE IN MY PRIVATE QUARTERS.
THE LAVISH FEAST INCLUDES CHOCOLATE FROM THE NEW WORLD!
I SEE YOU'RE TOO SMART TO WASTE TIME WITH THE LIKES OF THE FOUR INSEPARABLES.
ARE YOU SMART ENOUGH TO BE INTERESTED IN HELPING YOUR KING AND YOURSELF AT THE SAME TIME?

GO ON TO THE NEXT PAGE.

By the meal's end, you are faced with a choice.

WILL YOU . . .

. . . accept money to look for traitors among the Musketeers?
PLEASE TURN TO PAGE 41.

. . . accept but tell Monsieur de Treville?
TURN TO PAGE 107.

. . . refuse to become a spy?
TURN TO PAGE 96.

Your family wasn't religious, but you know anger is considered a sin. When St. Pierre really gets your goat, you duck into a nearby church to cool off. The beauty of the stained glass windows and the statues inspires you to draw!

You become so absorbed in sketching a statue that you do not notice the well-dressed woman approaching you until she says, "Not bad!"

Her clothes are even fancier than St. Pierre's. She is a countess and a patroness of the arts. She watches while you continue to draw. At first you feel self-conscious, but you are soon lost in the bliss of creation, filled with the statue's lovely serenity.

By the time you finish, the church's priest is standing next to the countess. Both of them are impressed by your drawing. The countess offers you a job drawing portraits of her family. The priest asks you to work for the church.

GO ON TO THE NEXT PAGE.

WILL YOU . . .

. . . accept the countess's offer to become your patron?
TURN TO PAGE 73.

. . . dedicate your art—and maybe your life—to the church?
TURN TO PAGE 86.

. . . refuse to let a bad start keep you from becoming a Musketeer?
TURN TO PAGE 68.

Exile is better than betraying those honorable men. You sneak out of Paris that night.

Father's insistence that you study languages helps you gain employment in Italy as a teacher. Since French is the language of diplomacy and culture, you work with powerful men and women. You marry well and raise a family.

Your life is happy, except for your secrets—and the fact that you can never see your parents and siblings again. You console yourself with knowing that at least you spared the lives of the Musketeers.

Eventually, you find out that they succeeded in freeing Jean-Pierre. You sometimes imagine what might have been if you had succeeded as a Musketeer and had joined with them in cheering, "All for one and one for all!"

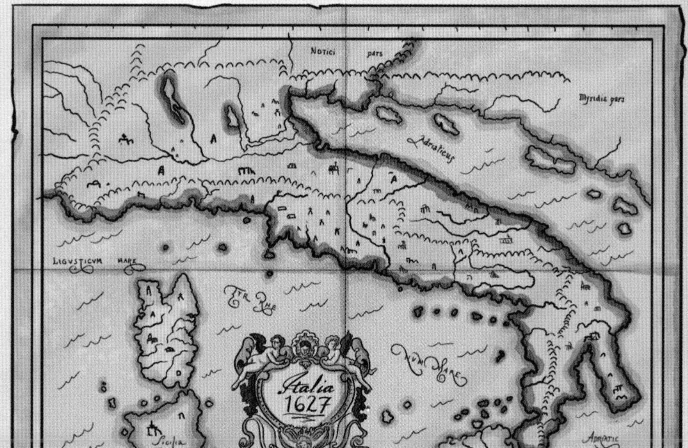
Notici pars
Adriaticus
LIGVSTICVM MARE
Italia
1627
Sicilia
Adriatic Sea

THE END

Porthos suggests a bet to make your duel of horsemanship more interesting. If you win, you gain a purse full of coins plus his recommendation to Treville that you be admitted directly into the Musketeers. Lose, and Porthos keeps your big, black horse. He leads you to a wide, grassy square, and the crowd follows.

In spite of being slightly spooked by the bright clothes and perfumed hairdos of the spectators, Pinky performs well. Then Porthos brings out muskets. You have never had a chance to practice with the Musketeers' namesake weapon. Porthos gives a sly smile. "Just pull the trigger and keep your seat. I'll demonstrate."

Porthos balances the musket between his mare's ears, then fires toward an empty part of the field: BOOM! Pinky rears, but you hold him tight, whispering, "It's just a loud noise."

You try to imitate Porthos's shot. But as the musket booms again, Pinky rears so quickly, you fall to the ground. Everyone laughs. Pinky runs off.

GO ON TO THE NEXT PAGE.

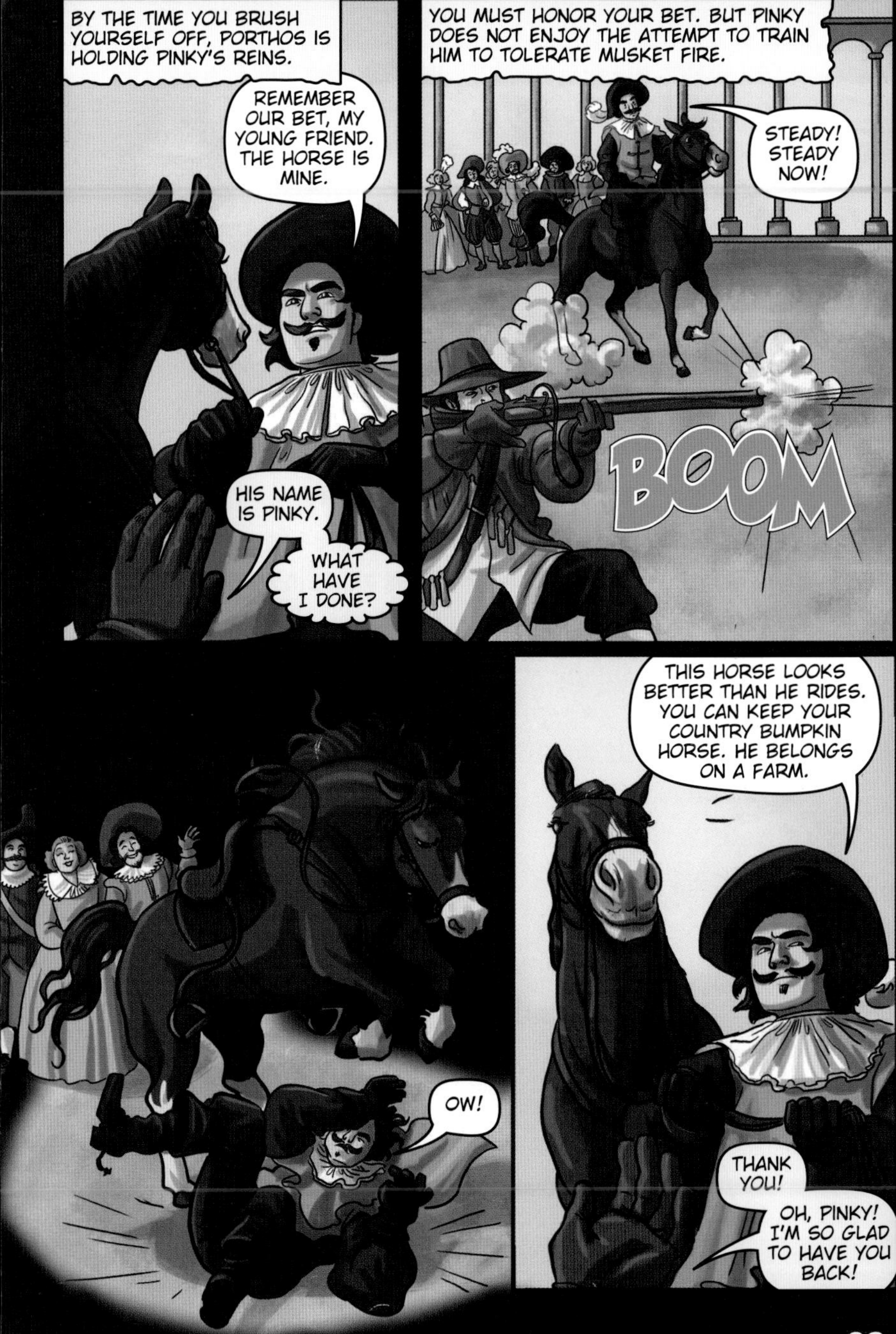
BY THE TIME YOU BRUSH YOURSELF OFF, PORTHOS IS HOLDING PINKY'S REINS.
REMEMBER OUR BET, MY YOUNG FRIEND. THE HORSE IS MINE.
HIS NAME IS PINKY.
WHAT HAVE I DONE?
YOU MUST HONOR YOUR BET. BUT PINKY DOES NOT ENJOY THE ATTEMPT TO TRAIN HIM TO TOLERATE MUSKET FIRE.
STEADY! STEADY NOW!
BOOM
OW!
THIS HORSE LOOKS BETTER THAN HE RIDES. YOU CAN KEEP YOUR COUNTRY BUMPKIN HORSE. HE BELONGS ON A FARM.
THANK YOU!
OH, PINKY! I'M SO GLAD TO HAVE YOU BACK!

TURN TO PAGE 50.

You search the grounds for tracks. But all you find are human footprints. You do find wolf hairs stuck to some brambles.

You make inquiries at all the farms that have been robbed. You find people living in poverty. Yet, they insist, they are better off than others who do not even have any land or livestock at all.

You have heard the expression "hungry like the wolf." Could a desperate man be responsible for these robberies?

"Ask the witch!" one housewife suggests.

Her husband seems ashamed of his wife's superstition. "That's just an old woman who lives alone in the woods."

"She's a witch all right," his wife insists. "She's got a potion for everything. Why wouldn't she be turning men into wolves?"

The farmer's beautiful daughter snickers. "Men are already wolves."

GO ON TO THE NEXT PAGE.

TWISTED JOURNEYS®

You and Giles reach the woods where the witch lives at sunset.

WILL YOU . . .

. . . seek shelter in the nearest farmhouse for the night?
TURN PAGE 104.

. . . bravely go on with your mission?
TURN TO PAGE 76.

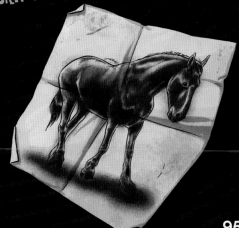

Rocheford politely accepts your refusal. But within days, he has you arrested for treason and thrown in the infamous prison called the Bastille!

Prisoners with money and influence can live very well there. *Your* cell mates include a family of rats and a man so filthy and starved you do not recognize him as one of Treville's troop. But Jean-Pierre recognizes *you*.

Like you, Jean-Pierre refused to turn into a spy. You remember when he suddenly disappeared. Since he was new and had few friends, everyone eventually concluded he had deserted and gone back home.

You stare into his sunken eyes and shudder. Is that what you will look like in a month?

But Jean-Pierre has an escape plan. Now that he has a helper, he's confident it will work. You don't want to rot with the rats or face a possible death sentence for treason. But can you trust the judgment of someone half mad with hunger?

GO ON TO THE NEXT PAGE.

WILL YOU . . .

. . . help Jean-Pierre in his desperate scheme?
TURN TO PAGE 100.

. . . beg an audience with Richelieu?
TURN TO PAGE 71.

You slip away from your troop, remove your uniform, and sneak into the village. You pretend to be a curious traveler so you can hear the peasants' side.

As a farmer's child, you understand what these people are going through. Sometimes Nature rewards hard work. But bad weather and taxes eat any profit like locusts, and the peasants often go hungry. Peasants cannot even hope for a better life for their children.

You haven't got much in your coin purse, but you offer it to them. You promise to talk to the marquis if they stop their rioting. The leader of the village finally agrees.

The marquis was not aware of the suffering of his serfs. When you explain the situation, he agrees to lower their taxes. He even agrees to build a school.

News of your success reaches Monsieur de Treville and then the King! They make you two offers: you may join the Musketeers or become a diplomat.

GO ON TO THE NEXT PAGE.

WILL YOU . . .

. . . become a Musketeer?
TURN TO PAGE 110.

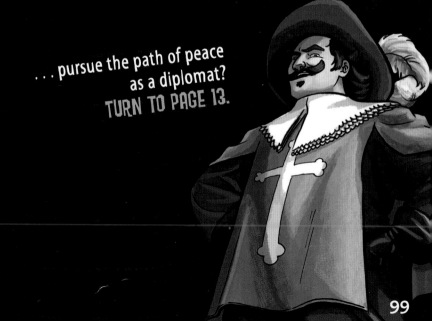

. . . pursue the path of peace
as a diplomat?
TURN TO PAGE 13.

Jean-Pierre's plan is for him to pretend to be dying. You call the guard and persuade him to bring a priest to hear the prisoner's confession and administer the Last Rites.

The prison's priest is an enormously fat man. Jean-Pierre believes that you can overpower him, take his robes, and carry Jean-Pierre wrapped around your waist disguised as the priest's giant belly.

At first you think the poor Musketeer has really gone mad. Then you see the priest and realize the plan has merit, especially if you use your skills as an artist to create a false beard out of Jean-Pierre's hair and threads from your tunic.

GO ON TO THE NEXT PAGE.

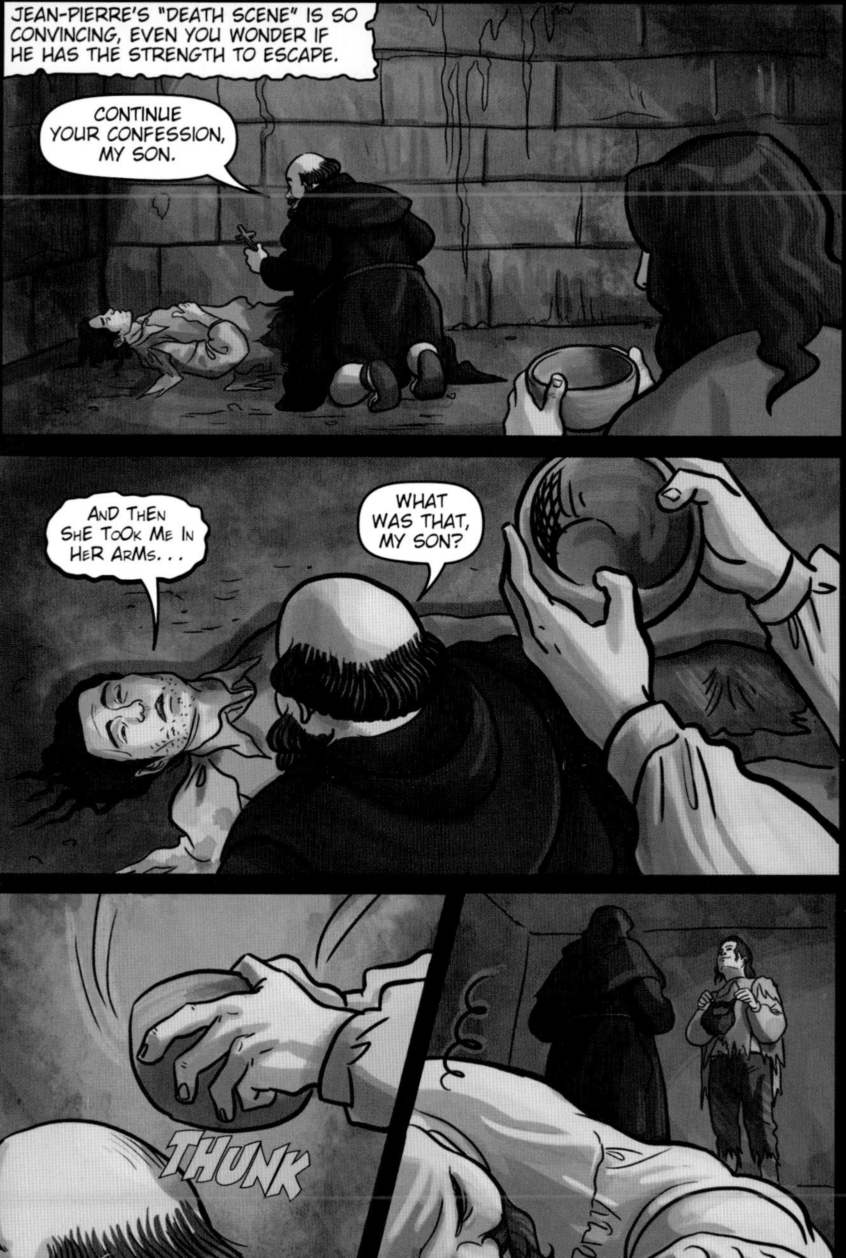

JEAN-PIERRE'S "DEATH SCENE" IS SO CONVINCING, EVEN YOU WONDER IF HE HAS THE STRENGTH TO ESCAPE.
CONTINUE YOUR CONFESSION, MY SON.
AND THEN SHE TOOK ME IN HER ARMS. . .
WHAT WAS THAT, MY SON?
THUNK

TURN TO PAGE 63.

You can't believe you wound up on the wrong side of a dashing rescue. Even worse, Richelieu blames Jean-Pierre's escape on your false information. You are arrested and put back in the Bastille!

How can you escape the death penalty? Perhaps your parents can pay a lawyer, or Father can beg Monsieur de Treville for help. You ask for paper, quill, and ink so you can write home.

But before you do, you have a nightmare in which your parents are hunted like foxes while all the Musketeers laugh. The dream fills you with fear. Maybe it's better if Richelieu doesn't find out who your family is. Maybe you should just make the most of however long you must live in this prison. At least your family will be safe on the farm.

GO ON TO THE NEXT PAGE.

When morning finally comes,

WILL YOU . . .

. . . write a letter home?
TURN TO PAGE 8.

. . . use the quill, ink, and paper to draw a plum
tree to decorate your cell?
TURN TO PAGE 28.

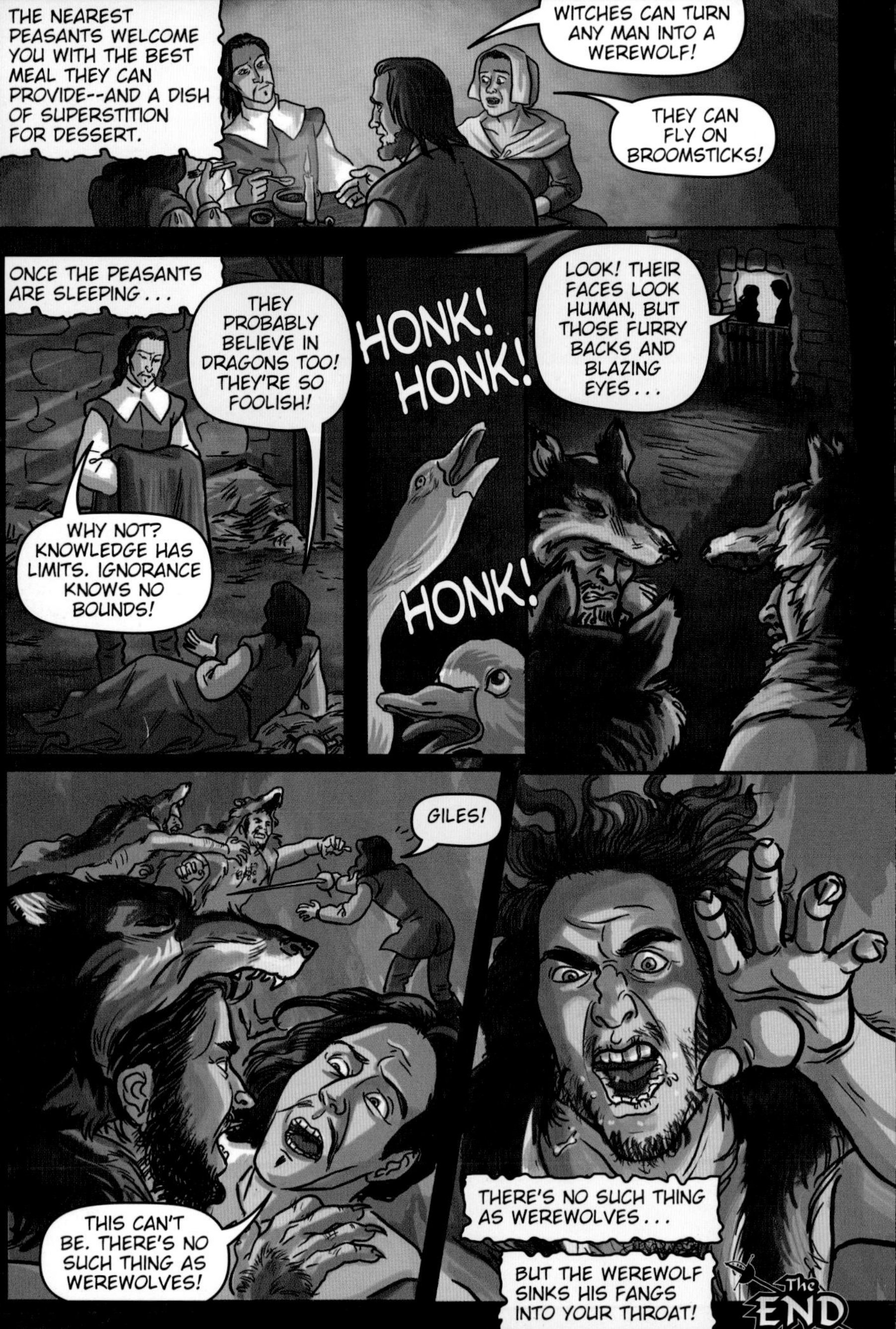
THE NEAREST PEASANTS WELCOME YOU WITH THE BEST MEAL THEY CAN PROVIDE--AND A DISH OF SUPERSTITION FOR DESSERT.
WITCHES CAN TURN ANY MAN INTO A WEREWOLF!
THEY CAN FLY ON BROOMSTICKS!
ONCE THE PEASANTS ARE SLEEPING . . .
THEY PROBABLY BELIEVE IN DRAGONS TOO! THEY'RE SO FOOLISH!
WHY NOT? KNOWLEDGE HAS LIMITS. IGNORANCE KNOWS NO BOUNDS!
HONK! HONK!
HONK!
LOOK! THEIR FACES LOOK HUMAN, BUT THOSE FURRY BACKS AND BLAZING EYES . . .
GILES!
THIS CAN'T BE. THERE'S NO SUCH THING AS WEREWOLVES!
THERE'S NO SUCH THING AS WEREWOLVES . . .
BUT THE WEREWOLF SINKS HIS FANGS INTO YOUR THROAT!
The END

Defeat seems certain. Then D'Artagnan leaps to your side and announces, "We Gascon bumpkins must stick together!" As Porthos rushes you both, Athos joins him. Then Aramis leaps to your other side.

While you are busy parrying and occasionally thrusting, the crowd grows. Then there is a sudden silence, and the crowd drops into bows and curtsies. The King is here!

Louis XIII is less than ten years older than you, but he has been king since he was nine. Louis rules as easily as breathing. You are awed by his attention, which gives you such great status that you are admitted directly into the Musketeers!

Your first mission is guarding the royal coach when King Louis goes to the countryside to hunt. You can't wait to write home to brag.

When the road winds through woods, Pinky's ears lie back. Porthos's hand reaches for his sword. You do the same as the trees come alive with would-be assassins!

GO ON TO THE NEXT PAGE.

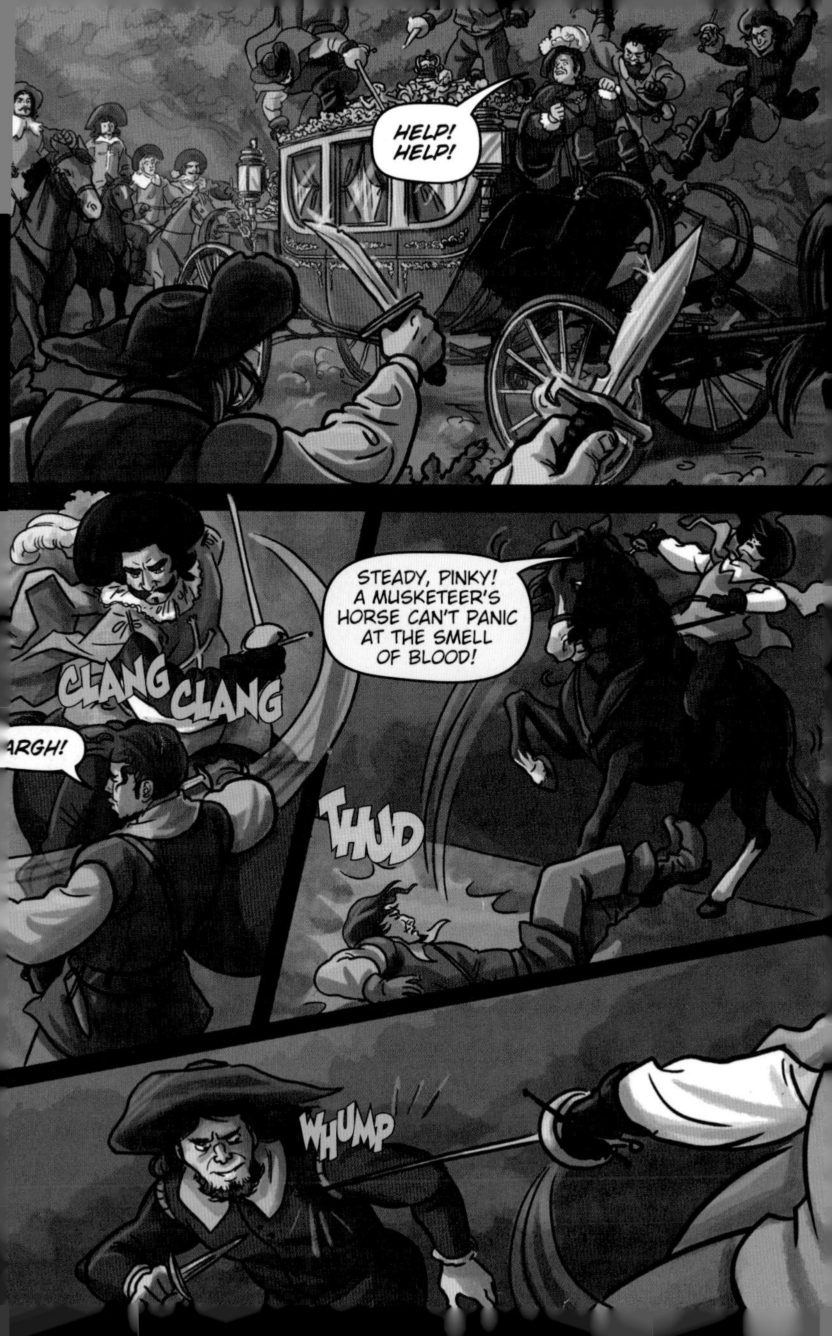
HELP! HELP!
STEADY, PINKY! A MUSKETEER'S HORSE CAN'T PANIC AT THE SMELL OF BLOOD!
CLANG CLANG
ARGH!
THUD
WHUMP

You agree to Rocheford's offer. But the very next day, you tell Monsieur de Treville. You suggest becoming a double agent.

Treville does not trust you. You are even more of an outsider than before, so you have no information to offer Richelieu.

After many lonely days, you realize your career as a Musketeer has withered. After a painfully long year, you go home.

Your parents have aged in your absence. They are grateful for your help on the farm. One chore at a time, you redeem yourself. By the time you marry and inherit the farm, you realize that being a Musketeer is not the only way to be happy.

You hide your sword under the floorboards of your barn. And when your child finds it, you exclaim with false wonder, "Now how in the world did that get there?"

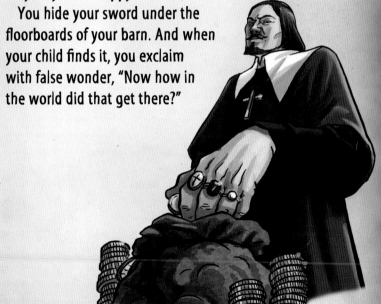

THE END

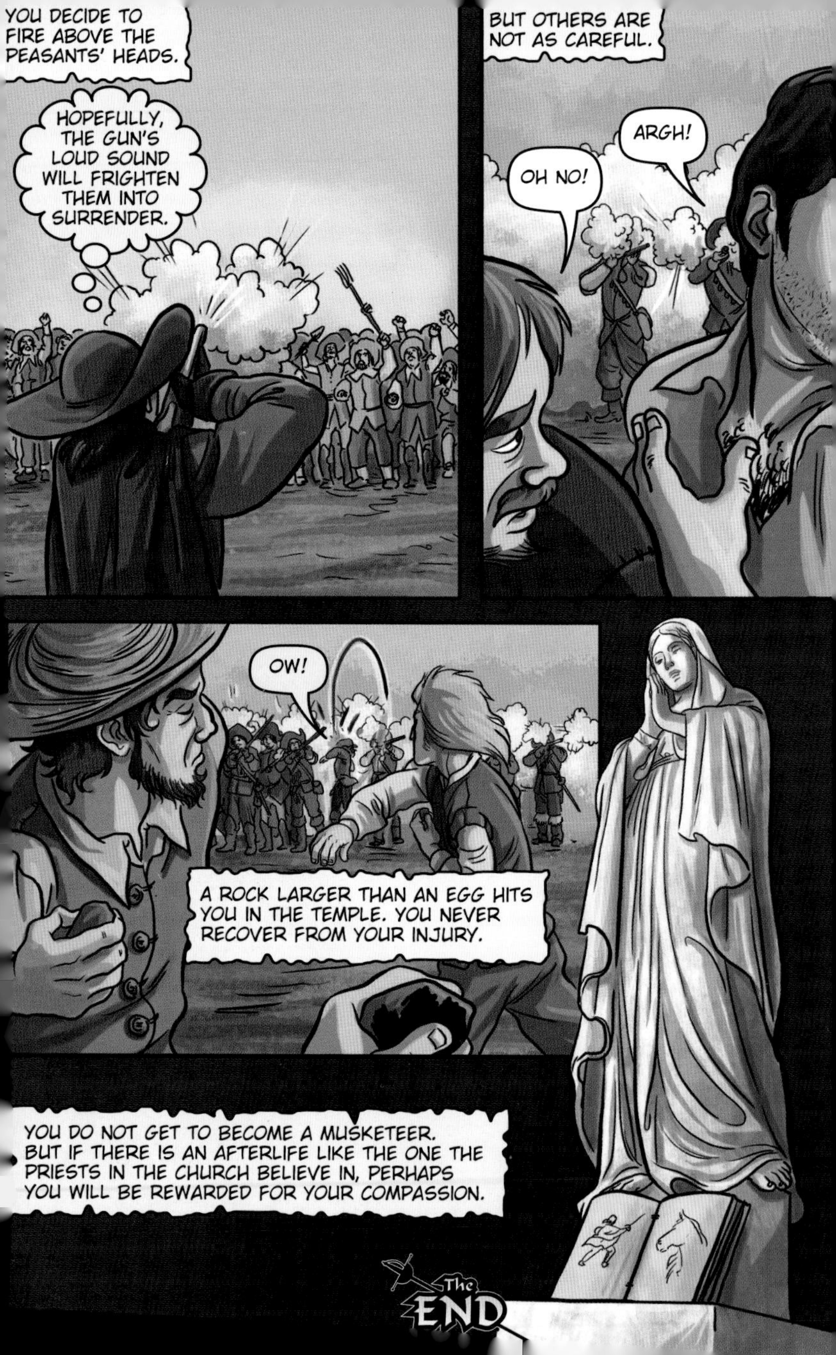
YOU DECIDE TO FIRE ABOVE THE PEASANTS' HEADS.
HOPEFULLY, THE GUN'S LOUD SOUND WILL FRIGHTEN THEM INTO SURRENDER.
BUT OTHERS ARE NOT AS CAREFUL.
ARGH!
OH NO!
OW!
A ROCK LARGER THAN AN EGG HITS YOU IN THE TEMPLE. YOU NEVER RECOVER FROM YOUR INJURY.
YOU DO NOT GET TO BECOME A MUSKETEER. BUT IF THERE IS AN AFTERLIFE LIKE THE ONE THE PRIESTS IN THE CHURCH BELIEVE IN, PERHAPS YOU WILL BE REWARDED FOR YOUR COMPASSION.
The END

Your meeting with Treville goes well. He agrees to let you train with him until you can find a position in a less important troop. You split your time between training and working for Spurs. To your surprise, you feel more comfortable in the stables than at Musketeer headquarters.

The horses don't care about status or money. They enjoy every day. In comparison, the Musketeers live in a constant whirl of intrigue, danger, and pointless competition with one another.

When Spurs offers to make you a partner in his business, you agree. You feel funny about having traveled all the way to Paris to become a stable manager. But you are as happy as a horse with fresh hay!

THE END

Finally, you are welcomed: you are a Musketeer!

Although you dreamed this would be a life full of adventures, the reality is very ordinary. Most of your waking hours are spent on drills or guard duty, watching for attacks that do not come.

You enjoy the friendships, although sometimes you are impatient with your friends' eagerness for battle. Does having *might* really make you *right*? To the annoyance of Porthos and the others, you and Aramis often have long, philosophical discussions about this.

When you reach retirement age, you realize your greatest triumph was your first battle when you found the courage not to fight.

THE END

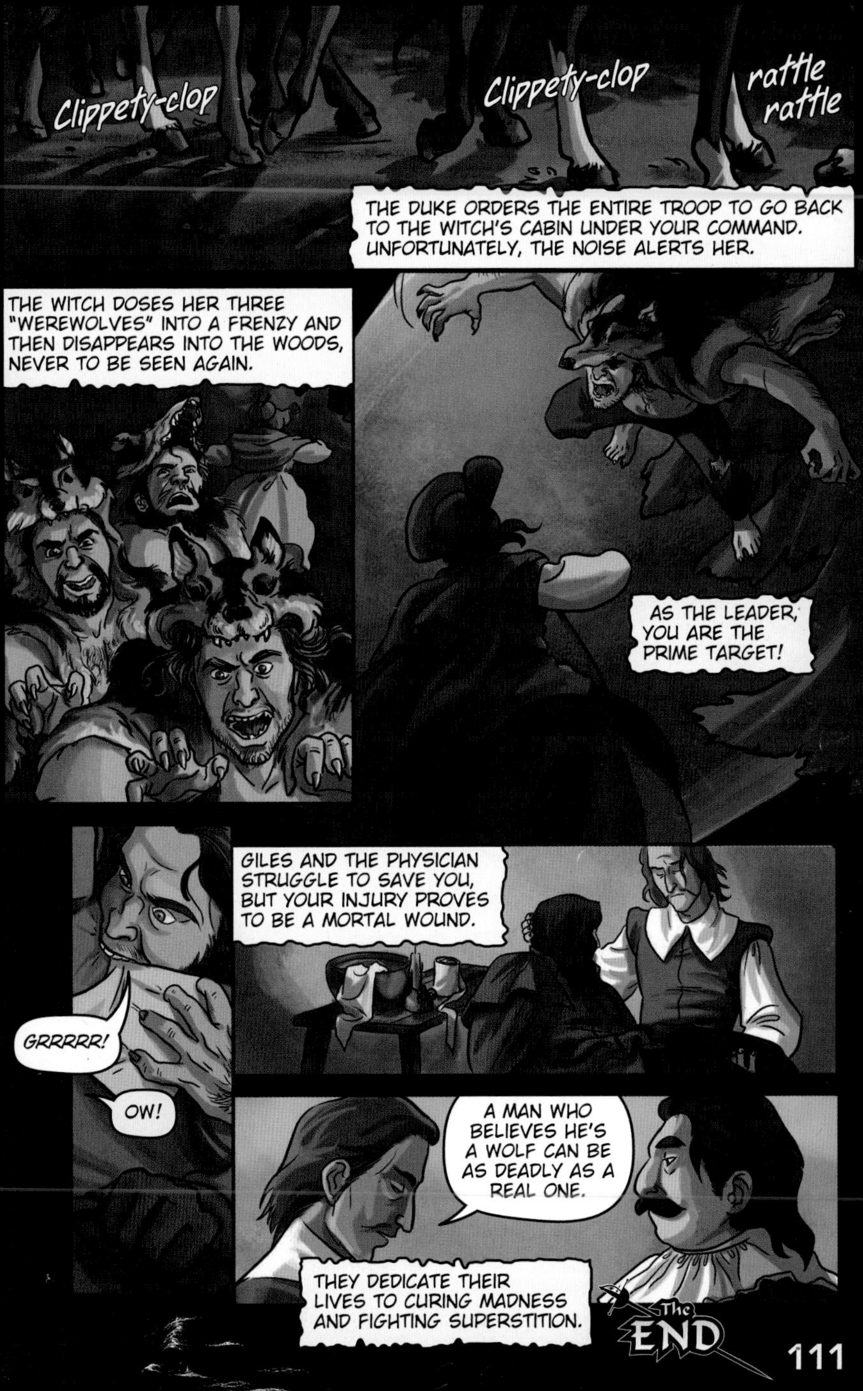

Clippety-clop
Clippety-clop
rattle rattle
THE DUKE ORDERS THE ENTIRE TROOP TO GO BACK TO THE WITCH'S CABIN UNDER YOUR COMMAND. UNFORTUNATELY, THE NOISE ALERTS HER.
THE WITCH DOSES HER THREE "WEREWOLVES" INTO A FRENZY AND THEN DISAPPEARS INTO THE WOODS, NEVER TO BE SEEN AGAIN.
AS THE LEADER, YOU ARE THE PRIME TARGET!
GRRRRR!
OW!
GILES AND THE PHYSICIAN STRUGGLE TO SAVE YOU, BUT YOUR INJURY PROVES TO BE A MORTAL WOUND.
A MAN WHO BELIEVES HE'S A WOLF CAN BE AS DEADLY AS A REAL ONE.
THEY DEDICATE THEIR LIVES TO CURING MADNESS AND FIGHTING SUPERSTITION.
The END

WHICH TWISTED JOURNEYS®
WILL YOU TRY NEXT?